W9-BRF-846

Old Ladies

Also by
Nancy Huddleston Packer

Old Ladies

Stories

Nancy Huddleston Packer

2012
John Daniel & Company
McKinleyville, California

"Night Noises," "Two's Company," and "Untangled" were first published in *Epoch*.
"Regulars," "Her Men," and "Dust Catchers" were first published in *Sewanee Review*.
"The Pioneer Women" was first published in *North American Review*, Vol. 287, No. 6.
"A Woman and His Dog" is scheduled to be published in *Cold Mountain Review*.

Copyright © 2012 by Nancy Huddleston Packer
All rights reserved
Printed in the United States of America

The interior design and the cover design of this book are intended for and limited to
the publisher's first print edition of the book and related marketing display purposes. All
other use of those designs without the publisher's permission is prohibited.

Published by John Daniel and Company
A division of Daniel and Daniel, Publishers, Inc.
Post Office Box 2790
McKinleyville, CA 95519
www.danielpublishing.com

Distributed by SCB Distributors (800) 729-6423

LIBRARY OF CONGRESS CATALOGING-IN-PUBLICATION DATA
Packer, Nancy Huddleston.
 Old ladies : stories / by Nancy Huddleston Packer.
   p. cm.
 ISBN 978-1-56474-527-9 (pbk. : alk. paper)
 1. Older women–Fiction. I. Title.
 PS3566.A318O53 2012
 813'.54–dc23
             2011045745

*For
Emily,
Will,
Charlie,
and
Julia*

Contents

Night Noises

FOR THE THREE MONTHS following Cal's death Louise kept hearing strange noises at night in the empty house. A file scratching metal, footsteps rustling on the stairs, sibilant breathing outside her locked bedroom door. She woke up several times a night and sometimes lay awake until dawn, listening to nothing.

"I'm getting dotty," she told her daughter, Sibyl, over the telephone. "I keep hearing awful noises at night, and I can't sleep. Cal always said I had an overactive imagination."

"Why don't you move up here to Seattle," Sibyl said, not for the first time. "I've found a lovely retirement community out on Lake Washington not fifteen minutes from our home."

"Well, I hope it's a good fifteen years from mine," Louise said.

Sibyl didn't laugh. Like Cal, she didn't always appreciate the joke. "Then why not get someone to live there with you?" she said and then gave a little gasp as though the idea had just come to her, which, Louise thought, meant she'd been pondering it for quite a while. "What about Dad's study? Private bath. Outside entrance. Perfect."

Louise didn't say anything for a moment. Maybe that could be the solution. She was worn out with all the noises, and she sure wasn't ready for a retirement home. "Well, maybe," she said.

EDWARD was the first to answer the advertisement Louise put in the *Palo Alto Weekly*. He was a small man with a pale unmarked face and lashless eyes and twig-like arms hanging from his short-sleeved shirt. Appearance seemed an unfair reason to deny him the room, so Louise told him that since the early bird gets the worm, he could have Cal's study. She chuckled to herself: he looked more like the worm than the bird.

He brought a microwave and a computer and some other machines she couldn't identify, and in his first and pretty nearly only words he said he worked at home, was that okay?

"He's a funny little fellow," Louise said to Sibyl after Edward had been there a week. "Not a speck of color in his face, not even a faded freckle. Never leaves his room. Never sees the sunlight. Just sits out there tapping on that computer."

"And the night noises?"

"Gone. The house is as silent as a tomb."

"Didn't I tell you?" said Sibyl. "Perfect."

"If you like the smell of pizza," Louise said.

Every evening Domino's delivered a pie that Edward microwaved for dinner and then breakfast and lunch the next day. Louise found herself sniffing to see what topping the pizza had. Sometimes she smelled spicy pepperoni, sometimes sausage grease, and sometimes the acrid odor of cooked olives.

One night lying in bed sniffing, she realized that the pizza fumes were invading her entire house, clinging to her curtains, seeping into her clothes, hovering like an invisible cloud ready to rain down cheese and tomato sauce and soggy crusts on her very own head. Edward had to go.

When Louise told Sibyl, Sibyl gave out a long-suffering sigh. "It made me feel better knowing you had someone with you, just in case," she said.

"Oh, if I croak, you'll be among the first to know." Louise laughed so hard she had to apologize. "I know you worry, I'll find someone who doesn't eat pizza."

SHE tacked the second advertisement on the post in front of the supermarket, where there would be no chance of Edward's seeing it. A furniture store deliveryman named Leo was the first to apply. Leo didn't look at all like Edward. He was overweight and soft, and his 49ers T-shirt was stretched tight over his belly, and his pants hung so low on his hips that the frayed cuffs dragged the ground under his heels. Probably sucked in that mammoth belly when his pants were hemmed. "I don't allow a microwave," she said.

"I ain't got one," he said, "so I guess we're all set."

The first afternoon after Leo had moved in, Louise was in her garden enjoying the sunlight and the late summer breezes, and reading the newspaper, when Leo walked up the path and planted himself on the edge of a lounge chair and said in his low, slow voice, "I know you been wondering how come I'm living here." Not for a moment had she thought of it, but she politely cocked her head to show an interest.

He told her he had moved out of his apartment and sold all of his furniture because it just crunched his heart to be there without his wife. She had left him, he said, for his old high school football buddy. "We were the grunts," Leo said, "him right me left upside the snapper." Louise had no idea what he was talking about, but she nodded sympathetically.

After that every day when Leo came home he took a seat on the lounge chair, folded his hands, and rehearsed his troubles with his wife. He was like a top spinning in a groove. The discoveries, the entreaties, the quarrels, his wife, his buddy, his buddies—for apparently the football buddy wasn't the first or even the second.

At first Louise found him touching and pitiable, and she was interested in his stories of lives so different from hers and Cal's, of people who acted on impulse and lived at the top of their lungs. But after three weeks of hearing the same litany of woes, she began to dread the sound of his footsteps. To escape one day, she slipped from the garden into her house as he approached. But he went to the front door and knocked and knocked until she answered. After that, wherever she was he sought her out. She knew it was her own fault for listening to him the first time. Now there was no escape without hurting the poor fellow's feelings.

And then one afternoon after Leo had lived there for five weeks, he came walking through the garden gate grinning. He told her that his wife had come by the furniture store and said she wanted to get back with him. Telling this, he looked sheepishly pleased, as though he had been the miscreant and had been forgiven.

"You'll love her," he said. "She's coming this weekend."

The next evening Louise called Sibyl and told her the saga of Leo and his wife and the buddies, and that now he wanted to install his wife in the study with him. "Next thing I know they'd both be spending their days telling me their disreputable stories and then squabbling all night, keeping me awake. I told him the room couldn't hold the two of them."

"Don't be too hasty," Sibyl said. "Maybe you could help straighten her out."

Louise blew out an indignant puff of air. "I'm not a social worker and I'm not a preacher and I'm not a policeman." She could almost hear Sibyl's disappointment wafting along the telephone wires. But she wasn't going to ruin her life just to save Sibyl five minutes of worry a week. "It would be worse than the pizza, worse than the night noises."

After a long silence, Sibyl said, "If you want me to come down to help you find someone suitable…"

"I think I'm capable of finding someone suitable," Louise said in a huffy voice. So she had made two little mistakes, so what. To cover her irritation, she changed the subject. "How're my little rascals doing?"

That set Sibyl off at once and she filled Louise in on her two daughters and Scouts, school, and soccer. "They'd love for you to come up for Thanksgiving," she finished, "and so would Ross and I."

During the years Cal was sick, Thanksgiving had been slices of turkey from the deli and a little can of cranberry sauce. It would be fun to help Sibyl prepare a real dinner and have a game of Scrabble with the girls. "I'll sure be there," Louise said.

She hung up the phone with a wry laugh. Imagine looking forward to helping someone cook and to playing games with two reluctant little girls. As a young woman she had dreamed of being an actress or a writer, something creative and special, but she had married Cal and moved to Palo Alto where he worked for Hewlett-Packard, and she had soon had Sibyl. Not exactly what she had yearned for, but a good life all told, far better than most people had. And Thanksgiving in Seattle would be a nice change, rain and all.

SHE thumb-tacked the next ad on the bulletin board at the university's housing office, pretty sure Leo wouldn't be looking there. The first to telephone was a woman named Ingrid Something-Scandinavian, who said she taught seventh grade at the local middle school. Louise didn't think a little female schoolteacher was much protection against the noises, and so she said the room was taken.

At three-thirty that afternoon, Ingrid Svendsen appeared at

Louise's front door. Her bushy hair was the color of raw pine and her face was round and flat as a plate. She was over six feet tall and her shoulders were broad, her hips were wide, and her legs, ensconced in purple tights, were thick and mighty. Louise thought maybe such a Valkyrie would be okay.

"The fellow I told you about changed his mind," she said.

"I figured as much. Show me the room."

Louise led the way into Cal's study, and Ingrid banged the doors and flushed the toilet and bounced on the bed until it clanged. When she stood up, she pointed at Cal's gallery of family photographs on the wall. "You'll have to get rid of those," she said. "Also these trinkets on the desk." She swept into her hand the little souvenirs Cal had collected on his travels.

"Now just a minute," Louise began. The pictures belonged on the wall, the souvenirs on the desk. Edward had probably not even noticed them, and Leo had said they made the place homey.

Ingrid turned her longshoreman's shoulders and brightly paint-ed moon face to Louise and her expression said nothing on earth could deter her so don't even try. "And I'll get a sack for those," Louise finished. She had always thought the trinkets were a nui-sance to dust.

WHEN Ingrid moved in on Sunday evening, a man helped her. "This is my boyfriend, Thomas," Ingrid said. "He teaches at the high school."

Thomas was a good six inches shorter than Ingrid, as wiry and twitchy as she was solid and planted. While they stood talking, he kept combing his fingers through his scraggly beard, and when he laughed—a quick nervous whistle through clenched teeth—he looked downright daffy. What a pair.

As Louise was preparing herself a cup of tea the next afternoon, Ingrid gave a quick little knock on the door that separated her room from the kitchen and barged right in. "Tea!" she exclaimed, plopping herself down across from Louise at the little kitchen table. "My favorite's Earl Grey, but I'll drink that stuff," she nodded toward the package on the counter, "if it's all you've got."

Louise frowned. What right had this woman to burst in uninvited and criticize her tea? But Louise didn't want to start off on the wrong foot, and so she covered her annoyance by shaking out a few more of the butter cookies she had as a snack every afternoon. Then she poured the tea.

After Ingrid had eaten three cookies and drunk the tea in two swallows, she leaned back in her chair and said, "Show and tell. What'd you do today?"

Louise shrugged. "Watched a few soaps, took my afternoon nap, read the newspaper."

"Soaps, naps, newspapers," Ingrid dismissed all that with a flick of her wrist. "Waste of time."

Now Louise was truly annoyed. "It's good to stay abreast of the news."

"Abreast of the news?" As Ingrid roared with laughter, her belly bounced in and out. "Don't you know you can't stay abreast of the news? By the time you finish reading one edition, everything's changed and you have to wait for the next. You never catch up. I want you doing better than that."

Louise was on the verge of telling Ingrid she had to leave right then, but she imagined having to admit to Sibyl that this one had lasted only one day. "Now it's my time to tell." Ingrid said an eighth-grader had been thrashing around out in the play yard with an iron pipe, scaring the hell out of the other kids, and Ingrid had wrestled it from him and dragged him by his ear to the principal's office.

"The kids cheered like hell." She wiped a cookie crumb from her chin and stood up. "You get a D-minus for show and tell." And back she went to her room.

That evening after a PBS nature show on the lives of cheetahs, Louise went to the kitchen. As she gathered up the dirty plates to put them in the dishwasher, she became aware of a moaning from the study, and her first thought was that if Ingrid had fallen she would never be able to lift her up. She'd have to call 911. Then she heard Ingrid say, "Oh, Thomas, you're so marvelous," followed by a few little yelps and then a deep loud groan.

Louise went straight up to her bedroom and sat down at her dressing table. Her face felt warm, and she was trembling a little. Were they…? Were they actually…? Surely not, with her in the next room. Ingrid probably had fallen and Thomas was struggling to pick her up. Or perhaps they were shifting the furniture. When people were moving something heavy, they did sometimes grunt.

THE next afternoon Ingrid walked into the kitchen, this time without even a single knock. "Earl Grey," she said, holding out a tin box with a painting of a Victorian woman sipping daintily from a teacup. "We've got to improve your palate." She thrust the little box into Louise's hand.

Louise was quite offended. There was nothing wrong with her palate or her tea. She was pretty sure that, Sibyl or not, Ingrid wouldn't last as long as Edward, let alone Leo. "I'll make tea with this, then," she said, allowing herself a tiny sarcastic twist to her voice, "unless my method isn't good enough for you."

Ingrid flapped her hand. "Oh, now," she said, "you're too nice to go all hoity-toity on me just because I don't like your tea." Then she laughed with such good humor that Louise felt a little ashamed, and so she smiled, to show she'd just been kidding.

Once they had drunk the tea and finished off the rest of the butter cookies, Ingrid rocked back in her chair until it creaked so loudly it seemed about to splinter. "I'll start the show and tell." She told Louise that a pushy mother had demanded that her daughter be given the lead role in the class play they were casting. "I said to her, You got one-half minute to get your butt out of my classroom if you want to keep it attached."

Louise gave a little gasp. "You said that in front of your students?"

"Boy did they have a good laugh watching her skedaddle. Especially her daughter." She broke off her laughter and eyed Louise suspiciously. "Your turn. I bet you watched TV and then read the whole damn newspaper including the want ads."

After lunch Louise had watched a female TV judge lambasting a frail, greedy old woman and had listened to a talk show with a bunch of goofy-looking wrestlers, and then she had taken the newspaper out to the garden. But she had certainly *not* read the want ads. "I certainly did not," she began in her haughtiest voice, but to claim credit for not reading the want ads would be demeaning, so she shifted in mid-sentence to "not read the newspaper. I read a book." Good grief, I'm telling a lie, she thought. But she was too far in to stop. Might as well push it a bit, show Ingrid her life wasn't just television and newspapers. "*War and Peace*," she said.

"Heard of it. Never read it," Ingrid said. "Tell me about it."

In the first year they were married, Louise and Cal had started to read the book aloud to each other but after three or four pages Cal either fell asleep or got amorous and then fell asleep. Cal finally admitted he couldn't keep the Russian names in his head, and they had not read past the second chapter, though Louise had always intended to go back to it. She said, "It kind of alternates. You know, war and then peace."

"I'm familiar enough with war, God knows, teaching kids," Ingrid said. "So what's in the peace section?"

"The peace section?" Louise repeated. She felt her face warming. How had she gotten herself into this mess? "Well, this Russian woman…"—she paused—"runs away with an army officer." Maybe that was *Anna Karenina*. Or Dostoevsky. She quickly got up and turned to the stove. "Want another cup?"

"Nope. What happens to them?"

"You mean the heroine and the…" She was pretty sure she'd said army officer, but she didn't want to take a chance. "…and her lover? They escape over the mountains to this exotic place."

"What place?" Ingrid asked.

And Louise fetched it out of nowhere. "Samarkand."

"That's a pretty exotic-sounding place all right." Ingrid stood up. "You get a C for today."

"Why just a C?" When Louise heard her own plaintive question, she felt the heat rise into her face.

"Reading a book is better than the newspaper but you sat on your backside all day. You're too young to just curl up and die." Ingrid drank off the last swig of tea. "Now you got to admit Earl Grey's a hell of a lot better than that swill you were drinking. Samarkand, huh? Never heard of it. See you tomorrow."

Her story deserved more than a C, Louise thought as she watched Ingrid disappear into the study. What a great touch Samarkand had been, but where on earth had it come from? Samarkand. Tamerlane. And then it came thundering out of the past. Right after the Soviet Union had collapsed, Hewlett-Packard had sent Cal out to investigate putting a new plant in Samarkand. She had been envious that he was going to such an exotic place, and she had asked him not to forget a thing.

When he came home, he brought her postcards of the rather shabby hotel where he had stayed and of the mausoleum where Tamerlane was buried. That was about it for Samarkand, he'd said— just shabby new stuff and beat-up old stuff. He had bought her a silk scarf from the tax-free shop at the Frankfurt airport. Yellow and blue with a chain design. She still had it someplace.

AS she finished supper that evening, Louise heard Thomas whistling. She decided that, just in case, she ought to let them know she was in the kitchen, and so she coughed as loud as she could. When she heard Thomas say, "O you beautiful doll, turn around so I can unleash those succulent melons," she banged her knife and fork on her plate and went to the sink and dropped in the frying pan with a bone-shattering clatter. But they seemed utterly oblivious of her presence. Ingrid began to ooh and ahh, and the bedsprings began to clang and Ingrid moaned, "Oh, Thomas, Thomas," and Louise ran out of the room.

"SHE has this little weasel of a man," Louise told Sibyl that evening. "I couldn't help overhearing. They made such a racket they drove me out of my own kitchen."

"People do make love, you know," Sibyl said, in her patient voice.

"Decent people do not carry on when others are within earshot."

"I guess people were a bit more secretive about sex in your day."

Louise resented that, as though her day were a thousand years ago. She said, "It's not the sex, it's the noise. The bedsprings like a brass band. And the moaning and groaning. I'm going to tell her she can't have him in the house."

"Suppose she leaves," Sibyl said. "This is the third one."

"Third, tenth, twentieth, I will not have my peace of mind destroyed by pizza smells or lovelorn fools or sex fiends."

When the heavy sigh wafted over the telephone wire, Louise knew just how Sibyl looked: eyelids at half-mast, lips pressed into a thin line, shaking her head just a bit, displeased but forbearing. Of course Sibyl was worried, and Louise knew it and regretted it and even appreciated the concern, and for forty-one years she had loved pleasing Sibyl. But Sibyl wasn't there to hear all that racket. Thomas had to go.

LOUISE decided she'd go last with show and tell the next afternoon, because hers was going to be the ultimatum: no Thomas or no You. When Ingrid came into the kitchen Louise couldn't help thinking about the noises the night before, and she felt herself flush. Ingrid didn't notice. She was too busy jiggling a little pink box by its string. "Still warm from the bakery. I thought you'd like a change from those boring cookies of yours."

Louise thought, Well, they aren't so boring you didn't eat practically the whole package. But she wanted everything to go well for the ultimatum, so she just tore off the string and opened the box. "Oh my, blueberry muffins. My very favorite." She set the muffins on a plate and poured the tea. "You're so sweet, Ingrid."

"I wasn't sweet to my kids today, I'll tell you," Ingrid said with a huge sigh. "Show and tell: I took twenty hyenas to the University's art museum. It was bedlam, chaos. I yelled at them so much the guard told me either shut myself and them up or everybody leave. My kids are hard to control. They're just at the age where their hormones are going off like Roman candles."

Last night, Louise thought, Ingrid's hormones had gone off like Roman candles. And Thomas's? Like firecrackers? Ingrid frowned. "You can laugh, but it wasn't funny at the time," she said. "Okay, your turn. Stay home all day?"

Louise was determined to rise to the challenge. "I went to the library." She hadn't really been to the library since she used to take Sibyl to the children's room where she had to sit in the tiny little chairs with her knees knocking against her chin. "I did some research on Tamerlane. He was the head man in Samarkand. Remember: *War and Peace?*"

"Well going to the library was at least better than sitting around all day," Ingrid said. "You know, I like carrot muffins better than blueberry. They're crunchier."

"I'm not finished with my story." Louise pressed her lips together and raised her chin.

"Sorry," Ingrid said. "What about this Tamerwho?" It was clear she wasn't the least interested.

"Oh, he's not the point," Louise said. "I saw a young man on the steps in front of the library. He was wearing blue jeans so raggedy you could see his skin through the holes."

Ingrid grinned. "I bet you followed him all around sneaking freebie looks at his bottom."

Louise drew back. "What an ugly thing to say."

"Why?" said Ingrid. "Was his bottom ugly?"

Ingrid's laughter was so cheerful, so abandoned, so rich and throaty that Louise could not help joining in. "He was pretty good-looking, actually," she said, "though I suppose he was a druggie. Only about sixteen."

Ingrid sobered at once and looked at Louise with a kind of pained wonderment. "Not much older than my kids. What happened?"

Louise said, "He looked starved and sick and so I gave him twenty dollars." Once outside a movie theater when she was a little girl, her aunt had emptied her change purse into a bum's filthy hands, and as the bum walked off Louise saw a dark stain on the seat of his pants and down his filthy pant leg. "The boy was so thrilled with the money that he wet his pants," she said.

"I'd sure hate to think of any of my kids out on the streets like that." Ingrid's face was flushed and her eyes filled. "It was awfully kind of you to give him the twenty dollars. Sometimes an act of kindness can turn a life around."

"Actually," Louise began. She didn't want to leave it like that, getting false credit for being generous and kind. "Actually," she repeated, but she didn't want to ruin the story either, "that's just what he said. He told me he was going to use the money for a bus trip home."

"You sure are a good woman, Louise." A car came to a noisy halt in the driveway, and Ingrid stood up. "There's Thomas."

And she was gone before Louise remembered to say, No-more-Thomas.

———

THAT evening Louise took her B, L, and T sandwich into the living room: one way to avoid getting run out of her own kitchen was to get out ahead of time. She turned the TV to the news on CBS. Something about nuns in Senegal, something about the side effects of a new drug, something about a senator and his secretary. I'd Rather not, she said and chuckling clicked to NBC and then on to ABC. Might as well have been the same handsome man reading the same news in the same portentous voice. She clicked to PBS. A man with shellacked hair spoke in sepulchral tones, and a woman with large square teeth kept interrupting him. It was amazing that she and Cal had listened every night to that boring stuff.

She turned off the television and took a bite of her sandwich. The bacon was cold and the lettuce was limp and the bread was soggy with tomato drippings. She might as well throw the thing away and get some crackers and cheese. Ingrid and Thomas were probably at it, but it was her kitchen, and she'd be damned if she'd be kept out of it.

And they were at it. Ingrid was groaning, and the groans became a shout and then a yelp, and Thomas's laughter vibrated like the cackle of a rooster. The proudest rooster in the barnyard, she thought. There was a long ooh and then Ingrid let loose a cannonade of joyous whoops. That little man causing that huge white body such frenzy, such turbulence, such pleasure. As Sibyl said, people do make love. Louise stood against the doorframe, listening. But when Ingrid shouted, "This is the best fuck yet," Louise went back to the living room and turned the TV on as loud as it would go.

Just think, a schoolteacher using that word. Not once had she heard Cal utter a four-letter word, even after he was non-compos when a lot of people would have taken the opportunity to let loose. She wouldn't tolerate having anyone talk that way in her house. Now it wasn't just Thomas but Ingrid herself who had to leave.

Louise knew Ingrid wouldn't just take the eviction the way Edward and Leo had—she'd demand to know why. Louise would have to make up some excuse—if she told the truth, they'd think she had been eavesdropping. She'd say she'd sold the house to a crazy Silicon Valley billionaire who was going to tear it down and build a fifty-million-dollar mansion. Or maybe that a long-lost brother had been found in a Burmese jungle and needed a home. Or maybe that she had been diagnosed with colon cancer like Cal's and was moving to Seattle to spend her last days with Sibyl. She'd think of something.

THE next afternoon Ingrid bustled in right after school, bearing a nosegay of blue and white flowers. "I saw this in the florist's window," she said, pressing the flowers against Louise's cheek, "and I immediately thought of you and your beautiful blue eyes."

Louise stepped back. How could she accept the flowers and then tell Ingrid she had to leave? "You keep them," she said. She covered the words with a conciliatory smile. "They'll look so nice in your room. You know: the blue blotter on the desk?"

Ingrid abruptly sat down and cocked her head. A film of dark cloud dropped across her moon face. "To reject the gift is to reject the giver. Have I done something to be rejected for?"

"Of course not." Louise grabbed the nosegay from Ingrid and hid her face in it. "They're lovely. It's just I don't want you to think you have to be bringing me things."

"Look here, lady, if I want to bring you a present, a little bit of a thing like you won't stop me, so don't try. Just go stick them in some water and I'll make tea this time." Ingrid patted the air as though calming Louise. "Now, now, I'm not saying it'll be better than yours." She roared out a laugh, and Louise thought that must be the way a lioness laughed.

Once they were seated at the table, Ingrid sagged back against the chair and sighed. "Sometimes it's hard to be a teacher."

She said that during one of those stupid state-wide exams, one of her kids vomited and ran out of the room and then all the kids sniggered and pretended to vomit and Ingrid had yelled that if they didn't shut up she'd swat them so hard across their chops they'd really vomit and one smartass said teachers weren't allowed to hit students and she had said, You want to bet, and he had said No and all the kids had shut up and gone back to the exam. They knew she wouldn't hit them in a million years, but they hated for her to be mad at them.

Ingrid's story had churned up a memory from a long time ago. Sibyl had been about six then and they were walking through the park when a woman nearby had slapped her little boy across his face. The boy had let out a blood-curdling scream and Sibyl had begun to cry. Louise had grabbed Sibyl's hand and raced across the park and straight home. "I drove in to San Francisco to Nordstrom this morning," Louise said, "to buy a birthday present for my grand-daughter, and I saw this woman slap her little boy right across his... chops."

"Some mothers ought to be shot," Ingrid said. "Where were you?"

Louise was startled. Was Ingrid trying to trap her? "Didn't I say Nordstrom?"

"Yeah, but I meant where in the store. You usually give me the whole picture."

"In the children's department." Louise had never been in the San Francisco Nordstrom—in fact, she hadn't been to San Francisco since Cal had been diagnosed—but she remembered an ad she had noticed in the newspaper though she wasn't sure which store—maybe Nordstrom, maybe Macy's, maybe Sears. "Right near a rack of blue and purple imitation fur coats for toddlers, if you can believe they'd sell such a thing." She paused to enjoy that nice touch. "Well, I certainly wasn't going to sit still for child abuse. I went right up to the woman and said, 'You shouldn't slap that little boy that way.' You should have seen the ugly look on her face."

"Wow. Catfight. So what'd she say?" Ingrid's eyes and teeth

lit up like jewels, and Louise knew she sure had her interest this time.

"She said, It's none of your…" Louise paused. "…fucking business." She had never said that word in her life and to cover her confusion she rushed on. "And I said, It is my fucking business because he'll grow up hating women and maybe rape my daughter, I mean, one of my granddaughters."

Ingrid gave a hoot of laugher and slapped both thighs, and Louise began to laugh, too. Yes, it was pretty funny, throwing that word back at the woman just as now she was throwing it back at Ingrid. It served them both right, using ugly words. And it did fit very well with her story.

When their laughter had quieted down, Ingrid glanced at her watch and frowned, "I have to pick Thomas up ten minutes ago. We're going over to Berkeley for the evening." She patted Louise's arm. "I just love our tea parties. If you ever want me to leave, Louise, you'll have to dynamite me out of here."

And could Louise then say, I have cancer?

When Ingrid left the room, Louise picked up the little glass vase with the nosegay. The flowers were lovely, so pretty and delicate. For the first year after she and Cal were married, he had brought her flowers every Saturday. She had been very happy that year. She had washed and starched and ironed his white shirts and brushed his dark suits and every morning sent him off like a warrior to do battle for Hewlett-Packard. A few years later when she was feeling neglected, she had asked him if now he took a weekly bouquet of flowers to HP. He had laughed hard at that, and soon she was laughing, and soon they were making love. But quietly. Not hollering and whinnying and braying.

"HOW'RE things going with the tenant?" Sibyl asked when she telephoned that night. "Still hot and heavy? Making out right this minute in Dad's study?"

This miffed Louise. "No, they're not. They're in Berkeley for the evening."

Sibyl said, "Ross thinks you ought to just tell her to leave if she's bothering you so much."

"What business is it of Ross's, please?"

That took Sibyl aback. "Well, he just thought that by now you're probably used to living alone and won't be bothered by the noises."

"Nothing wrong with a little noise," Louise said.

"But I thought that was why you were willing to have someone live there."

"Oh," Louise said. She had clean forgotten those other night noises. She sucked in her breath. "They might come back."

"Of course you could get someone else if you don't like her."

"I didn't say I didn't like her. She's very sweet. And every day we have wonderful talks."

Sibyl snorted. "About her sex life?"

"Not her sex life, Sibyl," Louise said in her testiest voice. "She tells me about school, and I tell her about my day. You'd be surprised at how much we have to talk about."

Sibyl said, "That's nice," a little condescendingly, Louise thought. Sibyl had always been a good daughter, no drugs or sex during her teen years, sent Louise's birthday present so it arrived on her birthday, telephoned regularly, did all the right things, but sometimes Louise had thought that the other side of that was being a little unimaginative. She got that from Cal. Louise reverted to her favorite change of subject. "How are the kids?"

"Great. Ross bought a new bright red SUV, and the girls are absolutely beside themselves. We'll be able to pack us all in for a trip to Mount Rainier when you come up for Thanksgiving."

"We'll have to see," Louise said.

THE next afternoon when Ingrid appeared with two chocolate éclairs from the French bakery, Louise clapped her hands. "What a treat," she said. "I don't think I've had such a luscious dessert in forty years."

As soon as they had finished the éclairs and tea, Ingrid launched into her show and tell. She said the principal had come into her classroom to evaluate her teaching can you believe his nerve. She had picked him up by the seat of his pants so his toes barely touched the floor and ushered him out to the hall and told him not to come back without a warrant. She roared with laughter. "Skinny nerdy drink of water. The kids loved it. Okay, your turn."

Louise said, "I was over at the shopping center." Since she went once a week for her groceries, talking about it wasn't nearly as risky as San Francisco, and so she launched right into a description. "All the windows are beautiful with lovely fall colors. Glorious burnt oranges this year and a deep rich green." She noticed that Ingrid was losing interest, and so she quickly shifted. "As I was waiting to cross over to the parking lot, a man stopped his bright red SUV right in front of me." She paused, pleased at how smoothly the story had begun, but unsure where to go next.

"So? What about him?" Ingrid asked. "Don't stop now."

And suddenly she saw it all so clearly. "He leaned out the window and looked at me and said, 'Girl of my dreams.' It's amazing, but I recognized him at once, though I haven't seen him in at least forty-five years. That's what he always called me. Girl of my dreams." She paused and smiled. "My first lover."

"Really?" Ingrid leaned forward. "When you were how old?"

Actually Cal had called her girl of my dreams, and he had been her only lover and the first time had been their wedding night when she was twenty-two. She couldn't remember whether she had told Ingrid how old she was when she married, and to be safe she said, "Seventeen. We ran off together when I was seventeen and he was nineteen. It was like a honeymoon."

"Wow! Romeo and Juliet." Ingrid raised her eyebrows and cocked her head. "Where'd you go?"

"He had a little black Ford coupe and we drove to Vancouver and took the ferry to Victoria Island. You know: Canada." She and Cal had driven his little Ford straight from Boise to Palo Alto and Cal's job, but Sibyl and Ross had gone to Victoria Island on their wedding trip. "We had a cabin right on the water and we made love among the sand dunes in the moonlight." She sighed. "It was the saddest day of my life when my father flew over from Boise and dragged me back home."

"What does the guy look like?"

"Slender, graying wings at the temples." She was sorry she had said that—such a cliché. She quickly added, "Still good looking but in the old days he was gorgeous." Louise had recently seen Tyrone Power in an old movie on cable and began to describe him. "Wore his black hair kind of slicked back—men did back then—and he had enormous brown eyes with lashes an inch long and a cute ski jump nose." Louise swooped her hand down her own nose.

"What did you say his name is?" Ingrid asked.

"Ross. Ever since then I've loved that name."

"Do you think you'll see him again?" Ingrid asked.

Louise couldn't keep the smirk off her face. "He's coming over this evening. The problem is, he's married." She drew in a breath. She hadn't really thought she'd take it that far. "But apparently not happily."

"My goodness, Louise, you're about to have an illicit affair!" Ingrid opened her mouth to pretend shock and then her laugh cannoned out. "Never too old, huh? Never too old. And I thought you were a dull old stick-in-the-mud when I first came here." She cocked her head toward the window. "Oh, damn, there's Thomas. Well, don't forget any of it, so you can tell me tomorrow in show and tell." She reached over and kissed Louise on the cheek. "You're really something, you know that? All that get up and go. Just full of beans. I'm so glad I found you."

———

LOUISE was preparing her dinner that evening when she heard Ingrid and Thomas coming home. She finished sautéing the salmon and took it and her salad to the little table where she and Ingrid had their tea. It would be only a matter of moments until she would hear the sounds of their pleasure, the clanging bedsprings, the oohs and ahhs, the moans and groans, all the delicious noises of the night.

Tomorrow when Ingrid came home with a rum baba or a slice of sacher torte, Louise would tell her the exciting story of Ross's visit. He was wearing blue jeans and a fresh light blue shirt, she would say, because that's the way he always dressed when we were young. Yes, she would tell Ingrid, it was as if we were still seventeen and nineteen and simply burning with desire for each other. It was wonderful, just wonderful, although—she imagined shooting Ingrid a shy little look—although I was afraid you might be disturbed by the noises. As she conjured up a vision of Ingrid, leaning forward, hooked, listening intently to every word, she felt alive, vibrant, full of beans.

Her Men

THEY WERE SITTING side by side in lounge chairs on the deck. Katherine had not been out on the lake in years, not since the old kayak had begun to rot, but on late summer afternoons while she drank her glass of wine, she liked to look across the smooth surface of the water to the island. But Jackie was spoiling the mood.

"You're always telling me I ought to get my life right, Gran," he was saying, "and here's my big chance."

Katharine sighed. "I thought the sixty-five thousand dollars two years ago was going to be your big chance." It was painful to be arguing, yet she would not give in to Jackie's latest wild scheme. "Few people get even one big chance, Jackie—almost no one gets more than one."

"Come on," Jackie said. "That was just bad luck." He cocked his head and crinkled his eyes at her, grinning, flirting, pretending to think she was only teasing, knowing that teasing was never her way. "This is a sure bet."

"A hundred thousand dollars," she said, "is a great bit of money to bet."

He laughed. "I'm not going to gamble it away in Las Vegas, Gran. It's going into this absolutely surefire marvelous deal. With Ralph. You always liked Ralph. Remember Ralph?"

She snuffled a laugh. "I'm not in my dotage yet. Of course I remember Ralph. He was the least unreliable of your friends, though far from the handsomest."

Jackie threw himself back in his chair and slapped his thigh. "Wait'll I tell him that. He was always scared to death of you. Called you the Iron Duchess." He laughed briefly, then straightened up and drew his brows together. "I know you don't know much about the Web and stuff like that, and really I don't understand it very well myself, so I won't try to explain it. But Ralph's company has this genius idea, something really great, and now he and his moneymen are about to take the company public. I'd double, maybe triple, my money once that happens. Ralph is doing me a favor to let me in early."

Who did you the favor the last time? she wanted to ask, but that would surely drive him away. "I'm no longer a rich woman, Jackie, whatever you think I might once have been."

"But it's just sitting there," he said, frowning with impatience, "making three or four percent if you're lucky."

"My dear, I live on that three or four percent."

"But I'll pay you twice that. This is a business deal, Gran, not a gift."

"Investing in some new-fangled something you don't really understand doesn't strike me as a very wise business deal."

Jackie sighed with exasperation and impatiently tapped his fingers on his knee. "Look, the money will be mine some day anyway, won't it? You can't take it with you, Gran."

"That's a nice thing to say."

He blushed and grimaced. "I didn't mean it that way."

"Oh? Well, what way did you mean it, Jackie?" She lowered her head to gaze at him over her glasses, waiting for an answer. She wanted him to be responsible for his deeds and his words. More muscle, less soft flesh. His sensible mother would have seen to that. "Say what you mean and mean what you say."

He abruptly stood up, the look of a petulant boy spreading over his face. "Then don't lend it to me," he said.

Even with his face flushed and his eyes flaring, he was immensely handsome. As handsome as his father. Almost as handsome as his grandfather. The same dark blue eyes, the full lips, the gold-blond hair, the skin tanned to copper. He was handsome, charming, and, she feared, quite useless. He had lived with her since he was eleven years old, when Gail died and sweet sad Jay had gone to drink and dissolution. He was Jay's only child. Her only grandchild. Her only kin.

"Oh, sit down, Jackie," she said, flapping her hand at him, "and explain to me exactly what the deal is, and I'll see what I can do."

JAY had come in very late. She had heard the boat thudding against the boathouse wall. Now perhaps she could sleep.

She had never been able to sleep while he was out, even when she knew that he would be late. At midnight she had gone out to the deck and listened. It was a calm night and the water and the wind were still. When she heard the dance music, the laughter, floating across the lake, she relaxed. The party was still going on, he was still safe. She had gone back to her room and read a trashy novel for an hour or so and then lain in the dark waiting. When she heard the kayak thudding against the boathouse, she turned off the light. She could sleep.

"Are you awake?" he asked, standing in her doorway.

"Yes, I'm awake." She sat up and turned on the bedside lamp. "Did you have a good time?"

"I guess. Okay if I come in?"

"Of course." She was pleased whenever he wanted to talk with her. They had always been close and had drawn closer after John had left.

The little bedroom armchair creaked with Jay's weight. He leaned his head back against the wall and closed his eyes. "Gail's pregnant," he said.

Katharine took a deep breath before she spoke. "Who?" she asked, though of course she knew. A local girl with black hair and almost purple eyes. Whenever Jay had brought her to the house, to pick up something, to leave something, he couldn't keep his hands off her. Katharine had known they were lovers, but she had thought it only a summer thing, that it would go away when he went back to finish law school. "That girl at the bait shop?"

"Gail. You know her name, Mom."

"Yes—Gail. Are you sure the baby's yours?"

He sat up in the chair, his eyes flashing. "That's an ugly thing to say. She's not a tramp, you know."

She knew no such thing. The girl was a tramp or she wouldn't be pregnant. But Katharine knew she had been foolish to be so blunt. "You're right to call me on that and I apologize. Pregnant. Poor little thing."

"Poor little thing she isn't. She's about the strongest person I know."

Yes, of course the girl was strong. Jay was the poor little thing, trapped like a rabbit, like a fish on a hook, like the stupid boy he was. "Does she know what to do, then? There's a clinic near Boston."

He flopped back with a sigh. "She wants to keep it."

Keep it. Katharine waited until her heart slowed its frantic pounding and she could trust her voice, and then she said, "That's rather foolish, isn't it? It would ruin her life."

"You mean mine. I guess I'd have to drop out of law school, at least for a while."

"No," she exclaimed. "No. You're both far too young."

"Twenty-three and nineteen. Age of consent. Old enough to marry."

She knew she had to move carefully—he could be childishly stubborn. "Old enough, yes, but wise enough?" she asked.

"Who marries wisely?" He cocked his eyebrow at her. "Did you?"

That didn't sting as badly as it once might have. Since John had moved to the other side of the world, Hong Kong, she seldom heard from him and now seldom thought of him. "I married wisely enough to get my precious son from it."

He smiled. "And you're afraid you'll lose him."

"I'm not thinking of me," she said. "I'm thinking of you and what being saddled with a shotgun marriage would do to you." Let him be angry—he needed to face the consequences, the ruin. "Tied to someone you don't love would destroy you, Jay."

"I do love her, very much, more than anything in the world. Even without this I would want to marry her, though maybe not until I got my law degree. Anyway I'm not as fragile as you think."

But he was fragile. More John's son than hers. "Let's talk about it tomorrow. You've stunned me with this news, and I need to sleep on it."

She lay wide awake in the dark. All her hopes for Jay smashed by his raging libido, his carelessness, falling into the clutches of a conniving girl who had set out to trap him. He was the girl's escape from summers selling worms and cut-up frogs and from cold barren winters with the Canadian wind roaring down the lake. Of course she had leaped at Jay. Kind, sweet Jay, and though the family was no longer rich, still well off, established. He was her ticket out, and she had caught him as deliberately as her father and brother caught the frogs and the worms.

Katharine awoke before seven and immediately went to the boathouse. She took down the paddle and unwound the kayak's tethering rope and pushed out. She kept close to the shore and paddled as silently as possible until she was beyond the point and would no longer be visible should Jay be up early. The current ran her way, and she did not need much effort to move the light boat along.

The bait shop was little more than a shack with one ancient gasoline pump on the pier. When Katharine's family had first come to the lake, there had been no need for a gasoline pump. The people who owned the summer houses had not wanted to shatter the silence with raucous noise and defile the air with noxious fumes. But now only the old-timers paddled their way around the lake. The young ones preferred motors. She had often wondered if the roar and speed made them feel virile and important.

The girl—Gail, Gail—stood in the open doorway of the shop, wiping her hands on a red cloth, watching as Katharine approached. She had on pale yellow shorts and a yellow windbreaker, and she wore a captain's cap pulled low. Katharine threw the kayak's rope around a post and drew closer to the pier. Gail started down the pier, but Katharine didn't wait. She did not want help. Helping would have given the girl an advantage. She hoisted herself up onto the deck.

"Need some bait for fishing, Mrs. Crandall?" Gail asked. She was pug-nosed and a bit thin-lipped, and her hands were black with grease. If Jay had to get himself in trouble, surely he could have done better.

"Haven't gone fishing since I was a little girl," Katharine said, with a smile. "The fish don't bother me, so I don't bother them."

"If they did bother you, I guess then you'd need bait so you could bother them back."

And with that, and the little ironic laugh that followed, Katharine knew that the girl knew why she had come. The two of them eyed each other for a moment, hard-eyed, only their lips smiling. "Is there some place we can talk?" Katharine asked, gesturing at a motorboat roaring toward the pier.

Gail threw the greasy red cloth onto the top of the trashcan and called into the shop, "Back in a couple of minutes, Pop."

They walked up the asphalt road until they came to a little path that cut back toward the lake. Gail turned down the path, and Katharine followed her. They soon came to a rocky promontory high above the water. On the near side the rock jutted back over a patch of sandy beach. Gail pointed to where the rock met the sand. "This is our favorite place—Jay's and mine."

Katharine looked at the shadowed overhang of the rock. Their little love nest. How tawdry. "Well," she said, "let's get down to business."

Gail cocked her head. "Is this about business?" she asked. She was small, smaller than Katharine, and wiry and quick. There was nothing shy about her, not even a tinge of that feigned subservience most of the locals showed the summer people. No wonder poor Jay had felt helpless. Katharine knew her plan would not come cheap.

"I suppose it gets rather lonesome up here in the winter," she began.

"We don't stay in the winter. We live in St. Cloud, where I go to the junior college." She smiled. "Fifteen thousand students, so it's not lonesome."

Katharine quickly picked that up. "Jay says you're a very smart girl. I wonder if a junior college could keep that intellect of yours occupied."

"Just say it, Mrs. Crandall. Say what's on your mind."

Katharine was surprised by the girl's impudence. Young people did not speak to their elders in that tone. Well, if blunt was what she wanted, then blunt she would get. "I'll pay for the operation and then three years at the state university, until you graduate. All expenses." And added, "And in the summer you could go to Europe, if you wished."

"But without Jay? That's the point, isn't it? I don't think I'd want to go to Europe or anywhere else without Jay."

Katharine felt the heat rise in her face. "If you care about him," she said, "you don't want to ruin his life. Burdened with a child, a wife. He's too young. You must see that."

"I don't at all. It could be the making of him, Mrs. Crandall. Taking responsibility instead of depending on his mother." Then Gail's eyes narrowed, and for the first time a look of uncertainty, doubt spread over her face. She leaned toward Katharine. "Did he send you? Did he tell you to say all that? To buy me off?"

Katharine turned away. If she said, Yes, Jay sent me, this proud girl would never forgive him, and that would put an end to this whole wretched business. She gazed out at the island in the distance, a mere speck against the far shore. It would be so easy. Yes, Jay sent me. But what good had lying ever gotten her?

"No," she said, facing the girl. "He didn't send me."

Gail's shoulders visibly relaxed. "I didn't think so, Mrs. Crandall. You see, I believe in him even if you don't."

"You're a very insolent young woman," Katharine said. "I came here in good faith with an offer to help you out of this"—she swung her arm toward the pier and the bait shop and the water glistening with oil—"awful place so you can make something of yourself."

"But suppose what I want to make of myself is the mother of Jay's child?"

"You're young, you're obviously intelligent. You surely don't want to ruin your life. You don't want to ruin his. What is it you really want? I'm not a rich woman, but just tell me and if it's within my power you'll have it."

"I already have what I want, Mrs. Crandall. Jay. And soon our baby. The man I love and the child I want. Wasn't that once all you wanted? It didn't work for you, but it will for me. And Jay." She peered closely at Katharine and then shook her head as though shaking off the encounter. "Now I need to get to work, if you'll excuse me. Pop can't do it all." She started up the path, and then turned back. She held out her hands, the nails rimmed black with grease. "I know they look a mess, but if you should invite us for Thanksgiving in Boston I'll clean them up. No one will know I'm just a grease monkey. You won't be ashamed of me, Mrs. Crandall, I guarantee that."

As Katherine furiously paddled back from the bait shop, her thoughts were roiled with what she would say to Jay. When she saw him standing on the deck, no doubt waiting for her, she veered off to the island. Before she spoke to him she needed to calm down, to think through an intelligent plan. She pulled the kayak onto the sandy beach and tied the rope around one of the pine trees. A cone had fallen to the base of the tree, and she kicked it as hard as she could into the lake. Then she sat down and lay back against the tree and began to take deep breaths, over and over again until her mind quieted, until reason returned.

It would be pointless to fight. She was no match for that girl. Not just the youthfulness and the sex, but her focus, her assurance. So formidable though only nineteen. If she alienated the girl— Gail, get that in your mind—she might lose Jay completely and that she could not bear. So what should she—what could she—do?

CLOUDS were swooping in from the northwest, and the lake's surface was quivering with the wind. But Katharine had spent every summer at this lake for thirty-two years, when her father had had

the cottage built, just before the Crash, and she was used to the
squalls that sometimes swept across. She was a strong woman, agile
and muscular, and even if the squall hit, she had to get away. She
couldn't bear to be in the cottage with John.

They had come to ready the cottage for summer, when Jay's
school was out and she and Jay would move to the lake and John
would come up from Boston for weekends. She turned the kayak
toward the uninhabited island a hundred yards away from the dock.
She was an expert kayaker and she was soon on the island. The
island was little more than a sandy beach and an acre of pine trees,
but as a child it had been her refuge from the parties and the quarrels. She glanced back at the cottage. John was standing on the
porch, his hands cupping his mouth. His words were lost in the
wind. Was he calling Be careful or I hope you drown?

Once she had fixed the rope around a tree, the memory she had
held back came rushing at her with such force that she dropped to
the ground. While John was in the attic taking out the deck furniture, she had seen the letter. It had not been addressed to her, but
she had thought it was from John's sister. That was unusual since
John had just spent the weekend at Carol's. Perhaps something was
wrong. John always shared his news from Carol, and so Katharine
had pulled the letter from the envelope. "My darling, the weekend
was glorious though much too brief." An odd way for Carol to start
a letter.

Katharine had turned to the second page to check the signa-
ture. "Yours forever if you want me, Richard." Richard? Richard,
yes. A good-looking young man she had once met when she came
upon him and John at a restaurant. A young associate John was
mentoring, he had said. And she had thought *How like John*. He
often had taken on as a protégé one of the firm's new young men
and had helped him to adjust. Helped them? The truth came thundering at her, and she felt that her head would explode. Of course

he had helped them, right into his bed. She had rushed from the cottage.

Alone now, on her island, she gave in to the images flooding her mind. There was John, naked, and lying beside him was that young man, Richard. The two of them were kissing, and then John's hand slid down to the young man's groin.

She pressed her wrist hard against her mouth. But she could not stop the awful sounds crashing through her body. They pounded against her belly, her chest, her throat. She dropped her hand from her mouth and gave in to the sounds, like an animal in pain.

At last exhausted, she rolled over and buried her head in the pine needles. The pungent odor of pine rose in her nostrils. Before they were married, she and John had often come out to the island in the moonlight and thrown their blanket over a bed of needles and made love to the sound of water lapping the shore. She remembered the delicious look of desire on his face, his moist lips, and his wide wild eyes. Surely that had not been faked. Surely there had been love, passion—for her. Surely their marriage had not been false from the beginning.

But perhaps it had been false and he had never loved her. Then why had he married her? Was it to have a cover, so no one would suspect? But did everyone know anyway? Was that why old Mr. Gore was so kind to her, with his mustache tickling her cheek as he kissed her? She had always thought he had pitied her because she was not beautiful as her mother had been. Now she wondered, had he known about John? Did everyone? John's partners at the law firm? Her golf friends? When she came upon Marilee and Betty sitting in the women's locker room, had they been whispering about her? The typical blind wife, the last to know. She had been a fool, refusing to see what was clear to everyone.

She began to cry again but then abruptly stopped. Was her anguish reduced to nothing more than the fear of humiliation? How trivial that was. She gripped her thighs and pressed her fingernails into the flesh. She had never wanted to be poor Katharine. She would not succumb now.

I want never to see you again, she would say to John once she was back in the cabin. Yes, that was the thing to do. Be straight and honest. Not crooked and deceitful as he was. What was worth keeping if you lived lies? Get out, she said to him. She saw his eyes fill, his mouth sag. There would be satisfaction in that, ejecting him from his home so that all the world would know. The world's opinion meant so much to him. That was why he had married her, a cover for his secret life—oh, yes, she had been a gawky plain girl, grateful to capture the handsome captain in his pinks, just home from the war. And, being grateful, being also a fool. What a fool, how blind she had been.

She stood up and began to unwind the rope from the tree. She felt very strong. She and Jay could get along quite well without him. Jay. What would he say when he was told why his father no longer lived with them? Would he be humiliated before his friends? So your Pop's a queer, is he? And Jay standing there, the tears springing to his eyes, his full lips trembling with shame. He would be devastated. She had not prepared him for disgrace.

She gazed across the lake. All the lights were blazing, even in the boathouse and the attic, John showing he cared about her and wanted her safe. He had always been thoughtful. Yes, it was true. Flowers on every occasion, special gifts—last year for their anniversary an antique gold pendant watch, with *Forever* and their entwined initials engraved inside the cover. And, when he was out of town, he called every evening, as he had last weekend. Last weekend, yes, pretending to be at Carol's. He probably had called her so that she would not call him and find him not where he said he would be.

Her breath caught and her belly hardened and the tears began again. But then she said, *Just stop. Stop stop stop. What's done is done.* Yet what was she to do? What would she do about Jay?

And then it came to her. Nothing. Of course. Do nothing. Nothing had changed except her knowledge. He was still John. Her husband. Jay's adoring father. A good man. He loved her, she knew that—his kindness, his interest in her life—she had just not known the limitations of that love. Really, she had lost nothing. Nothing that she had ever actually had. If she said nothing and did nothing, nothing would come of it. Oh, she knew she would have dreadful moments when evil images swarmed into her mind. But John need not know and Jay need not suffer.

The sky had darkened and the clouds had begun to roil. Across the lake the porch lights were flashing, on off, on off. Come back, come back. And, when she got home, he would admonish her in his quiet way. *Really, Katharine, this is not the weather for water sports.* She cupped her hands in the frigid water and washed away the remnants of her tears. Then she unwound the rope from the tree and kicked off from the island. She paddled against the gathering whitecaps, toward John, toward the lies she would live for the rest of her life.

"I hope you weren't worried," she would say, perhaps kissing his cheek. "The lake was so beautiful with the storm coming that I couldn't resist watching it from the island. You know what a fool I am."

KATHARINE had been forbidden to take the kayak to the island without a life jacket. But the stiff old jacket interfered with her paddling, and it smelled sour. There was no one to see her if she didn't wear it. Her mother would sleep through the morning, and her father never arrived from the city until late afternoon. She really didn't need the jacket. Her father had taught her to handle the kayak, and now even he said she was an expert.

She lifted the paddle from the wall and freed the ropes and stepped into the kayak. She loved kayaking, lifting and twisting the paddle, dipping the blade into the water. Pushing off from the boat-house ledge was always the best moment. Floating free of the ropes, free of the boathouse, free of all the troubles.

As she paddled toward the point, she glanced back at the house, and remembering the night before, she felt her face crimsoning as it had then. Now she wished she had just let that drunken man drown. She had been in the boathouse trying to read *Oliver Twist*—the party had made so much noise she couldn't read in her room, and she needed to get at least one more chapter read before her fa-ther came the next day. When she heard the splash, she had come out onto the dock, and there was the man, floundering in the water, his head banging against the piling. She had caught the man's shirt collar and begun to scream and three men came running from the house and pulled the man from the water.

When it was clear the man had only swallowed water and would be all right, Carl—whom she hated most in all the world—said she had saved the man's life, and he lifted her onto his shoulders and paraded her around the deck, singing, "See, the conquering hero comes, sound the trumpets, beat the drums." It had been horrible, humiliating.

Her mother had taken her from Carl. "Can't you see she doesn't like that," her mother said. Her mother leaned down and there was the perfumy smell of gin on her breath. "Come on, I'll take you up to bed, sweetheart. You don't need to read that silly old book tonight." They had gone up to Katharine's room in the attic and her mother had lain down on the bed with her and had promised she would stay until the sandman arrived. When Katharine was almost asleep, Carl had come to the door and her mother had left and then Katharine had stayed awake for at least an hour, maybe two, and listened to the laughter downstairs.

As the house disappeared beyond the point, Katharine vowed that the next time her mother had a party, she would go straight to her island so she wouldn't know if someone fell off the dock and was drowning. Even though it was wrong to wish people to die, she wished they would all fall in the lake and would drown, especially Carl.

The sun had just emerged from the stand of pines on the far shore and was slowly burning the mist off the lake. The only sounds were the wind rippling the lake water and the rhythmic splashing of her paddle. It was the best part of the day. Yet her mother and father never saw the lake like this. Why had they built the lake house if her mother just drank and had parties and her father only came out every ten days or so and then stayed so briefly that it seemed he just wanted to check that they were still alive and the house had not blown away. He and Katharine had not gone fishing once all summer.

She pulled the kayak up onto the island's beach and wound the rope around the trunks of three tiny pines her father had had planted. Last summer she had tied the boat to a single trunk, and when a big wave came along the tree had been almost uprooted. Her father helped her stamp down the roughened dirt around the roots until the tree looked just like the other little twiggy pines.

The island was her special place. There was a lot to do there, if you used your imagination. Once she had made a fortress out of driftwood. Once she had collected pine needles and shaped them into a necklace, though it had split apart before she could get it home. Sometimes she just roamed around pretending she was Robinson Crusoe or Friday, practicing how to survive if she were shipwrecked. She didn't feel like an adventure today, so she decided she would collect some of the tiny water-smoothed stones and polish them until they were as shiny as jewels and perhaps make a necklace.

By the time she had found enough pretty stones, the sun was halfway toward noon, and her mother would be waking up. She quickly untied the kayak and pushed off from the beach. Then she saw her father standing on the deck in his light seersucker suit and his Panama hat. He would be angry with her for not wearing the life jacket. Though her heart was beating hard, she managed to smile and wave as she coasted into the boathouse.

Once she had tethered the boat, she came up on the deck. "I'm sorry, Poppa," she said. "But I was extra careful."

"I'm sure you were, but it's dangerous and the rules still apply." He paused. "At least the rules as far as you're concerned. But never mind that for now." He held out his arms and she came into them. "How's Poppa's girl?"

"I'm fine," she said. She knew she had to say something else— it was rude to answer in monosyllables. "I'm going to polish these rocks and make a necklace." She pulled a handful of the rocks from her pocket.

"I'm glad to hear you have projects and aren't just idling away the time here."

"No, Poppa, I'm not idling."

"And have you continued with *Oliver Twist?*"

"Yes, Poppa. I'm nearly at page eighty."

"I'm pleased with that, Katharine." He sighed heavily. "I imagine you're rather tired from the party, aren't you? When the dreaded cat is away." He shook his head. "Your mother doesn't seem to realize we're in a depression and money's scarce."

"Oh, yes she does." Her mother was standing in the doorway in her nightgown and robe, her tangled hair hanging every which way. "This may be the tail end of the whoopee days, but I intend to enjoy them as long as I can, and I won't let Mr. Gloom ruin that."

Poppa put his hand on Katherine's head. "Why don't you go

to your room, Katharine, and start on that necklace. Or, better, go work on *Oliver Twist*."

"First a good morning kiss," said her mother. She leaned over and kissed Katharine on her forehead and ruffled her hair. "My sweet girl. Did you sleep all right?"

"How could she have?" her father said in a harsh voice.

As she climbed the steps and went into her room in the attic, Katharine heard their voices rising and falling and rising again, though she couldn't make out the words. She picked up *Oliver Twist* and carefully removed the little clip her father had given her to mark her place in a book. It was silver and it had a large K at the top.

She opened the book and ran her eyes over the first line and then the second and the third. Though she knew each word, putting them together didn't make sense. She began again at the top of the page and read word by word, slowly. Her mother thought the book was too old for her, but that wasn't it. She was a very good reader and had read books much harder than this one. But these words were just marks on the page.

Why had they married? Had they liked each other then? She thought of the picture in their bedroom in Boston, her mother so pretty in a white lace gown that came to her ankles and her father handsome in his striped long-tailed coat and funny shoes with the covers over them, both grinning and so happy. If she hadn't been born, would they still be happy? If she went away, if she lived on her island, would they be happy again? She went to the window. They were sitting in the lounge chairs, facing the lake. They were no longer shouting, and though that was good, she wanted to hear what they were saying. She lay down on the floor beneath the window so that if they looked up they wouldn't catch her eavesdropping. But she couldn't really hear them no matter how hard she strained. She closed her eyes.

"All right, little one, wake up. The floor is hardly a place for a nap."

She quickly pulled *Oliver Twist* from under her shoulder. "I'm awake, Poppa," she said.

"Now you are." He reached for her hand and pulled her up. "Perhaps Dickens is a little too much for you." He took the book from her and straightened the bent pages.

"No, Poppa, I like it."

"Good. I thought you would."

"I'm glad you came early," she said. "Can we go fishing?"

"Not this time. I'm going right back to the city, but I want to have a little talk with you. You're a strong girl, Katharine. Off kayaking and hunting rocks by yourself."

"I'm sorry, Poppa, I won't go without the life jacket again."

He flicked his fingers, dismissing that. "No, no, that's not what I'm talking about." He sat down on her bed and motioned her toward him. "This will be very difficult for you," he said, once she was standing at his knees and he was holding her hands, "but I want you to be very grown up and strong. Promise?" He waited until she nodded and then said, "Sometimes people make mistakes, and the proper action is to rectify them as soon as possible. Your mother and I agree on that if little else." He pulled her toward him and held her head against his chest. "Do you understand what I'm telling you, little one?"

"Yes," she said. "I understand." She clenched her hands and held her elbows tight against her ribs. "Can I go over to the island now if I wear the life jacket?"

SHE listened as Jackie revved the car's motor and roared up the gravel driveway to the road. And then there was only the sound of the water sloshing against the piling. Every summer since she was a child she had come up to the lake. Once a drunken man had broken through the railing and fallen into the water, and she had somehow saved his life. She looked out at the island and the pines her father had planted, now grown so tall. She had made love on the sandy beach. She had collected pinecones and stones, and she had often hidden there.

Should she sell all this so that Jackie could have the money? It might be the making of him, and if not perhaps she wouldn't know.

Charade

WHEN SHE HEARD the motorcycle skittering to a halt on the gravel driveway, Helen quickly dropped the trowel and stood up from the flowerbed. She was wearing shorts, and she didn't want whoever to see her with her rump in the air. The driver cut the engine and jerked the motorcycle onto its stand. A stranger.

"This Number Four Opossum Road?" the man asked. When Helen nodded the man started toward her. "I saw the ad for a handyman down the road at that Jake guy's deli," he said. "Job still open?"

The man was about her age, somewhere in his fifties, stubby ponytail, worn T-shirt with the 49er logo, jeans stiff with oil and whatever. "I don't think I've seen you around here before."

"I'm from over Madrono Valley."

Madrono Valley was on the other side of the hill from the ocean, a collection of RVs and dilapidated houses, broken cars in the yards and a raucous roadhouse flashing beer signs. All the local crews were busy readying the other summer cottages for the season. She only had this weekend to finish the job—on Monday she had to be back at the college to teach her classes—and there were gutters to be unclogged, the overgrown field mowed, mice nests to clean out of the carport, a dozen other chores before the place went on sale. She was relieved that someone had seen her ad. And this fellow was big and looked strong-bodied, and he probably needed the work. "Is thirty an hour okay?"

"Sounds about right." The man reached past her and with his thumbnail scratched a patch from the salt-coated window. "You live here?"

"Yes. I'm selling it."

"Too lonely, huh?" He gestured at the houses sparsely scattered over the field and down the cliff. "Not much to do for fun."

Fun? Perhaps she had been too quick to hire him. "Maybe not fun," she said, "but there's plenty to do for work. You can start out there." She pointed the trowel at the waist-high grasses in the field around the cottage. "Can you use a scythe?"

The man cocked an eyebrow and said, "Lady," in a disgusted voice.

"Not everybody does, you know. You'll find one in the carport." She turned away and then turned back. Maybe she had been too abrupt, rude. "What's your name?" she asked. "In case I need to call you."

"I've been called Heyyou and Lookee-here and a lot worse," the man said, grinning, "but my friends call me Eddie."

She laughed at that. "Okay, then, *Eddie*, if you get thirsty there's a hose bib behind the carport."

As Eddie walked past her toward the carport, she looked down at the marigolds and petunias still to be planted. The agent had told her she should spruce up the outside with flowers. But she wouldn't kneel and bend over again with this stranger around. The flowers would have to wait. There was plenty else to do. She climbed the three steps to the porch and went on into the kitchen.

The burned grease on the oven walls looked like a diseased growth, a melanoma, maybe. It had been accumulated over years of sputtering fat and little fires as she and Lamar had broiled steaks and chops together. She found the oven cleaner under the sink and began to spray it on the hardened crusts.

A harsh screeching sound came from the carport, and she looked through the back window. Eddie was bent over with a pocket knife, scraping the blade of the scythe, cleaning off the petrified grass and mud left on it the eighteen years she and Lamar had owned the cottage. When he looked up, she nodded approval and went back to spraying. She had been right to hire him—he, at least, knew how to work.

When the fumes began to burn her eyes, she closed the oven door. Let the stuff do its job. She took two wine boxes down the hall to the guest bedroom to divide the books that had made their way up from the city. When she had first met Lamar, she had discovered that each possessed a worn copy of *Middlemarch*, and that had made her think they were truly soul mates. So much for literary taste. She sat on the floor in front of the bookcase and reached for a book. Was it a *his* or a *hers*? Hell with it. She'd give them all to Goodwill, along with the other discards. If Lamar had wanted his books, he should have taken them with him. She quickly emptied the shelves.

On the way back to the kitchen, she stopped and gazed out at the craggy cliffs and the Pacific swelling in the distance. Her happiest days had been spent here, just the two of them, hiking down to the rocky shore, reading while they listened to Verdi and Mozart, making love to the sound of the sea. Though it was more than her fair share, Lamar had insisted she take the cottage as her part of the settlement. That was like Lamar, thoughtful, generous, and a little patronizing. After a year of lonely weekends, spinning incessantly on her loss, on Lamar and his betrayal, she realized that being in the cottage only worsened her misery. Though leaving was wrenching, she knew she had to move on.

She glanced over at the field. Eddie was mowing away, his shirt off and the sun glistening on his back. An immense tattoo spread like a giant spider around his shoulder and arm. When she peered closer, she made out a yellow sunburst with thick jagged red and blue rays. Why would he brand himself that way, leaving an ugly smear across a perfectly nice body? Perhaps a tattoo was a mark of belonging in Madrono Valley, as a good haircut or well-kept fingernails might be for the summer people.

The ringing of the telephone broke through the stillness, and she went into the kitchen and picked it up. "I'm at Jake's Deli," Lamar said. "I heard you were selling, and I want to pick up some of my stuff. Okay?"

Apparently he thought he could just show up without warning. But there was no point in letting herself be angry, in telling him off. It was over, and whatever wounds she had needed to inflict surely she already had—most of them on herself. "You're just in time," she said in a cheery voice. "I'm getting everything ready for the movers."

"Well, I'll give you a couple of hours this afternoon. I figure since I helped make the mess, the least I can do is help clean it up." He spoke in his joking voice, expecting her to be amused

"I really don't want…" she began. But rejecting his help would only expose how wounded she still felt. "…you to think you have to, though I could use a strong back."

"What do you say I have Jake make us a couple of sandwiches?"

"I say great. Sure beats another bowl of corn flakes." Remembering Eddie, out in the sun, mowing away, probably ravenous, she added, "Make that three and a six pack of beer."

THE oven cleaner had done its work, and with a handful of paper towels she wiped off the black slime. Then she started cleaning out the refrigerator, loading the garbage can with half-empty jars of mustards and pickles and jellies. The orange marmalade, a Lamar favorite, had hardened into stone. She tossed it into the garbage sack. The dregs of a marriage.

At first she and Lamar had been disappointed not to have children, but they had come to see it as a blessing. Couples they knew had racked up debts they couldn't even calculate, paying for cures for their druggy children. Her own nephew was catatonic after a skateboard accident, Lamar's niece suspended in a haze of powerful pills. Being childless had at first made her and Lamar very sad, but they knew they had been saved from the real heartache. And they had time and money to enjoy the good life. Self-centered, yes, and that had often bothered her, but they drove hybrid cars, recycled bottles and newspapers, reused their grocery bags, and at the end of the year made large gifts to their favorite charities.

She had finally come to realize that in her smugness she had been blind to Lamar's discontent. When he confessed that he had fallen in love with a new associate at his law firm, she had tried to joke it away—these little infatuations are like adult male mumps, she had said, painful, dangerous in the rare case, but you'll survive. When she realized that she had lost him, a desperate fury boiled up, and evening after evening she spewed scalding words over him—and lay awake regretting them, knowing they were driving him further away.

Once Lamar had moved out, her fury collapsed, and she gave way to months of despair, hardly able to teach her classes, feeling worthless, discarded like a pair of Lamar's worn-out shoes or a shirt with frayed cuffs. At last she thought that if she sold the cottage, breaking the final connection, surely she would return to her old self.

SHE had finished wiping out the refrigerator and had begun to wrap the dishes when she heard Lamar's car rolling up to the carport. A moment later he was standing in the kitchen door. "Hello, Helen," he said. His expression was kindly and remote and a little wary, the face he had shown her over the past year as though she were a volatile neighbor to be placated at the mailboxes. "Nice to see you."

"You, too." See how cool I am, her smile said.

"So you decided to sell." He set the sack of sandwiches on the counter and stuck the beer in the refrigerator. "I guess real estate is doing pretty well around here."

"So the agent assures me."

"Well, I hope you make a fortune. What can I do? Find me a job. Anything."

She smiled at that. He was wearing his usual summer look— blue oxford button-down, pressed khakis, white Nikes, blond-gray hair clean and crisp. She could not imagine him out in the sun like Eddie, whacking away at the grasses. He had done the mowing that first year, but after that they had hired a local crew to do the spring clean-up. "Pick out what you want to take back with you, and then I'll find something."

He went down the hall to the guest bedroom, and she heard him rummaging through the Goodwill boxes, humming and half-singing the toreador song. She picked up a handful of newspapers and went back to wrapping plates.

"I GUESS I'll go to the deli and get something to eat." Eddie stood in the doorway, drying his head and neck with his shirt bunched in his hand.

"We have some sandwiches and beer here if you'd like them," she said.

He raised his eyebrows. "Well, now, you're what I call a real nice lady. Thanks." He tossed his shirt out to the porch railing, and washed his hands at the sink.

Lamar came into the kitchen. "Oh, hello. I thought I heard a man's voice."

"Eddie's helping me fix up the place for the sale," Helen said, "and Lamar is...we're divorced," and quickly added, "Time for lunch."

The two men followed her into the alcove off the kitchen and sat down, and she emptied the sack of sandwiches onto the table. "Roast beef," she said, picking up one of the sandwiches. Lamar's favorite at Jake's. Pickles and mustard, caramelized onions, lettuce, and tomato. He was smiling at her, so confident, so sure of himself, so sure of her. "I bet you'd like this one." She handed the package to Eddie. When she felt rather than saw Lamar's smile vanish, she felt confused, uneasy. No, she told herself. Don't fall back into that old trap of making things right for Lamar. "Take your pick, Lamar," she said. "Tuna or egg salad. I'll get the beer."

As she opened the refrigerator, she heard Lamar say, "So you're a friend of Helen's?"

"You could say that," Eddie answered after a pause.

"Known each other long?"

"Not too long."

"You live around here?"

"You're asking a lot of personal questions," Eddie said.

"Sorry," Lamar said in a startled voice. "I don't mean to be intrusive."

"And I don't mean for you to be," Eddie said.

Chuckling silently, Helen took the six-pack from the refrigerator. The clever lawyer put on the defensive by the likes of Eddie Heyyou. Good old Eddie.

She didn't know she was going to do it until she was doing it, but as she came around the table, she lightly brushed the six-pack across the sunburst on Eddie's shoulder and smiled at him when he glanced up. She freed one of the cans from the pack, pulled off the tab, and handed the can to Eddie. Then she set the six-pack on the table and motioned for Lamar to help himself. That's how it began, the deception, the pretense, the little charade. Let Lamar think there was someone else in her life, some other knight being chivalrous. He needn't know it was for a price.

As they ate their sandwiches and drank the beer, she addressed most of her talk to Eddie, frequently touched his arm to emphasize a point or underline a joke, and then turned to say something to Lamar as though suddenly remembering his presence and her manners. Lamar responded in monosyllables and registered his irritation with disdainful glances from her to Eddie.

Eddie seemed very pleased with the attention and laughed and talked easily, about his motorcycle, about a ride down to LA with a buddy who owned a Harley. When Eddie had finished his sandwich, Helen shoved half of hers over to him and insisted he eat it even though it was just egg salad. Eddie said it was good egg salad because it was made by a good egg named Jake. He took a bite of the sandwich and talking around a mouthful said, "Jake was on the Snake's old Raiders team."

"Snakes? Snakes play football?" Lamar said, springing suddenly to life. "Baboons, maybe, gorillas, certainly, but snakes?"

Eddie hurried the last of the egg salad down with a swallow of beer. "You never heard of Kenny Stabler? The Snake? Never noticed his picture behind the cash register at the deli? 'To my old pal Jake who saved me from a ton of pain'?" He cocked his head at Lamar and narrowed his eyes, as though summing him up. "I'd say sports ain't your thing, right?"

Helen knew Eddie had touched a boil. Lamar had never been athletic and had always felt a little uneasy when other men talked about sports.

"I prefer different forms of entertainment," Lamar said. "For instance, music, opera." His voice was a little haughty and his chin rose in defiance, a show of false assurance Helen knew very well. For a moment she thought of intervening, then decided to let it play out.

"Opera? Those big fat women going *lalala*?" Eddie dismissed that with a laugh and a wave of his hand. "Not me. I like rock, Pearl Jam, that kind of music. Opera sure ain't my thing, I'll say that."

"I would never have thought it was." Lamar waited a moment for that to sink in. "Helen and I had season tickets to the opera and thoroughly enjoyed it. Didn't we, Helen?" He leaned toward her, nodding, his expression complicit and insistent. It was true. They had gone on Sunday afternoons and sat in the front row of the Grand Tier, and she had loved it as he had—though she had sometimes thought it was because he had.

"I've reverted," she said. "I'm back into rock." She smiled at Eddie and stood up. "No more dawdling, you guys. Back to work."

"Yes, ma'am, boss," Eddie said with a salute. She reached over and flicked her fingers against his tattoo.

When Eddie had gone back to the field and Helen was gathering up the sandwich wrappings and beer cans, Lamar leaned against the kitchen door frame and, jerking his shoulder toward the field, said, "What's that guy's name again?"

"Eddie."

"Just Eddie?" Lamar asked, his voice impatient. "No last name?"

"Williams," she said, shoving the mess into the garbage can. If she'd had time, she might have come up with something unusual, not so obvious. "Edward H. Williams." H for Heyyou.

"The two of you, I don't know." Lamar shook his head. "I mean, I'm not a snob or anything, but he doesn't seem to be your type."

"My type? What's my type?"

"I mean, he's just…" He raised his hands at the difficulty of

coming up with acceptable words. "He just doesn't seem very intel-
lectual."

"I guess I'm going in for the more physical type now," she said.
"I've always had a secret yen for the hard hats."

"You never told me that."

"Would I have told you?"

Obviously annoyed, he walked to the window and looked out
to where Eddie was working. "And that tattoo?" He swung around
to face her and puffed out a sneery laugh. "So now you have a yen
for tattoos?"

"I think that one is quite beautiful," she said. "It's a sunburst,
the perfect symbol for Eddie. Energy, vigor, vitality. Isn't he wonderful?" And indeed she felt quite wonderful herself, to think all
that up.

Lamar's lips tightened. "I can give you about three more hours.
Then I have to get back to the city. Where should I start?"

THROUGH the afternoon they worked, Lamar washing the windows with wet newspaper, Eddie hacking away at the grass, Helen
finishing up the kitchen. When she saw that Eddie was almost finished with the mowing she took a cold beer out to the field. Lamar
was working on the front windows and she felt him pause as she
passed.

"Once you've finished here, would you mind going up on the
roof and clearing out the gutters," she said to Eddie. "There're garbage bags in the garage you can use for the muck."

"You afraid I'd dump all that nasty stuff on your pretty head?"

"What? No, of course not, but I don't want you to throw it
down on the flowers."

"Yes ma'am, boss. Hey, lookee. The ex is sure giving us the
eye."

She glanced at the porch where Lamar was dipping a handful of paper into the bucket of soapy water, his head cocked so he could see her. Let him get a good look. She pressed the cold can against the tattoo. "Here, this is for you. Let me know when you finish the gutters."

As she walked back into the cottage, she glanced at Lamar. He had turned back to the window, but she could see the sullen droop of his lips and disapproving set of his jaw, and she felt elated.

AT a little after five, Lamar stuffed the soggy paper into a garbage bag and threw the dirty water down the toilet, gathered up some books and CDs and reclaimed a favorite windbreaker from the Goodwill box. He came to where Helen was wrapping cups.

"I wish I didn't have to go back to the city," he said. "I hate to leave you when there's so much to do. I could maybe come back tomorrow."

"Thanks but Eddie's very good help." She pointed upwards where Eddie was rattling the gutters.

"Physical work, maybe, but since you're planning to sell, you need somebody who knows something about business."

"How do you know Eddie doesn't?"

"Come on, Helen, it's obvious. He couldn't possibly know how to deal with the agent about his percentage or negotiate with the bank, stuff like that." He smiled. "After all, I am a lawyer."

When he moved closer to her, she could smell his familiar odor, the ironing smell of his crisp shirt, the after-shave he used, his fresh sweat. He put his hands on her arms and slid his fingers up the wide sleeves of her blouse, and she saw in his eyes the delicious look she had once known so well. "Would you like me to come back tomorrow?" he said in a husky low voice, moving his thumb across her armpit toward her breast. "I still care for you, Helen. Very much. You don't just wipe away all those great years we had together."

"Oh?" she said with an ironic laugh. "I thought that was exactly what you did." She pushed him away. "It may come as a devastating surprise to you, Lamar, but I don't want you to come back. I don't need you. Eddie is quite enough."

A dark flush rose into Lamar's face. "Well, I hope you'll be very happy," he said.

"I already am." Though she knew that in the pain-inflicting game she hadn't come anywhere near even with him and never would, she felt better than she had in a long time.

LAMAR'S car had hardly reached the crest of the hill when she heard Eddie clomping down the ladder. She was pleased he had finished cleaning out the gutters so quickly, and since there was still enough light he could sweep out the mice nests in the garage.

Eddie came into the kitchen. "He sure took his sweet time leaving," he said in a voice full of disgust. He took a beer from the refrigerator and rolled the cold bottle over his forehead before popping off the cap. "I sure don't figure a sexy babe like you with a wimpy guy like that."

His tone, his words—the crudeness, the impudence—shocked her, and it took her a moment to find her voice. "I'll get your money."

As she walked past him toward the living room, he set his beer on the counter. "Forget that," he said, grinning. "We got more important things to be doing." He reached out and put his hand on her arm.

"Get your hands off me." She whipped away from him. "Don't you dare touch me."

His grin turned quizzical. "What's going on?'

"What indeed," she said. "I'll get your money and then I want you out of here."

The grin washed out of his face. "I don't get it."

"Surely you can understand plain English, can't you? I'll get your money and then I want you to leave."

She made a move toward the door, but he stuck out his leg to block her. "Hey," he said, his voice plaintive, "you came on to me, you made a pass at me."

"Don't be ridiculous." He couldn't be drunk on a beer or two. Was he crazy? "How could you possibly think such a thing?"

"You been after me all day," he said. "I seen you watching me out the window and then rubbing my tattoo every chance you got."

"Rubbing your tattoo? I wouldn't touch that ugly thing with a ten-foot pole."

"You saying you didn't?" He reached his hand across his chest and patted the tattoo as though pointing it out to her. "Come on, you did so."

She stared at him, at the tattoo spreading across his shoulder, the acid yellow, the dull, sickly blues and reds. Touch that? She let out a little scornful laugh. But then she saw herself out in the field, smiling up into his face, and yes, touching the beer can to the tattoo, touching him. And Lamar had seen her and she had had her little victory. "Well, okay, maybe, once, maybe," she said in a softer voice. "But I'm afraid you misinterpreted."

Eddie looked puzzled, confused. "What do you mean, misinterpreted? Misinterpreted what?"

"What I was doing. It really had nothing to do with you."

"Nothing to do with me? That don't make sense. Who did it have to do with?"

"Lamar," she said. "It was just a game I was playing with Lamar."

"A game?" Eddie's eyes flashed and his lips rolled back tight against his teeth. "I'm a football for the two of you to kick around?" He hammered his chest with his fingertips. "I'm a fucking football?"

"Of course not." She patted the air to calm him. "No one was kicking you around. You simply misunderstood."

After a pause he said, "Yeah, I misunderstood all right. I should of figured you wouldn't be coming on to me. I ain't fancy enough for you. I ain't got no season tickets at the fucking opera. I ain't nothing but a stupid handyman. Right?"

"Of course not. Look, I'm very sorry if your feelings are hurt. I certainly didn't intend that. But what more can I say?" She shrugged to show that should be the end of it. "I'll get your money. Thirty dollars an hour, wasn't it?"

As she started past him, he grabbed her shoulders and swung her around against him, and the stench of his armpits poured over her face. "You had your fun," he said. "Now I want mine." His face was flushed, swollen with rage.

A sound like a waterfall began to roar in her head. "I'm so sorry. Please don't hurt me," she said, in a high cracked voice. And then she was stumbling back against the sink.

"Don't look at me like that," he shouted. "Jesus. I ain't going to hurt you. Just give me my fucking money."

When she realized he had shoved her away, that he wouldn't hurt her, relief spread through her with such a rush that her legs began to tremble. "Thank you," she whispered.

She lurched past him into the living room, pulled open the desk drawer, and fumbled out her wallet. When she heard his footsteps behind her, she swung around to face him, as though that might hold him off.

But he wasn't looking at her. With his head averted, he walked past her to the porch door and braced his forearms against the doorjamb. He was breathing heavily, the tattoo rising and falling. Now what?

After a moment, he said, "I'm sorry for grabbing you, and I don't blame you for being scared." His voice had lost its furious edge. "But I ain't like that. I wouldn't never do nothing like what you were thinking. It's just I saw red there for a minute."

And charged like a bull, like the animal you are. Pay him, she told herself. Get him out of here before he sees red again. "Let's just settle what I owe you." She cleared her throat to settle her voice. "Eleven to after five? Six and a half hours?"

"It wasn't okay me being rough with you." He turned to face her, shaking his head as though puzzled. "But that game you were playing?"

"We don't need to talk about it." She drew the wad of bills from her wallet. Six times thirty plus fifteen. "Does one ninety-five sound right?"

But he wouldn't let it go. "It just kind of got to me. Like you and him think you can treat people like me any way you want and it's okay. Like I ain't no better than a pile of dogshit you stepped in."

As she began to count out the money, she heard the echo of his words. No better than a pile of dogshit you stepped in. Was that what he had said? That she thought people like him were no better than dogshit? No wonder he had been loud, threatening. She stopped counting and looked over at him. With his cockiness and anger gone, what was left was a look of hurt and shame.

A wave of anguish swept through her. She had done that to him. To win the puny victory over Lamar, she had humiliated this man—this rough man from Madrono Valley—had made him feel like dogshit. She wanted to tell him that she wasn't like that, that she had not intended to hurt him any more than he had intended to hurt her. It had happened because Lamar had come swaggering in, so on top of the world, so full of himself. That was why she had played the little game—to hurt Lamar. And she would tell Eddie she knew how it felt to be treated like dogshit because Lamar had treated her that way.

"When Lamar left me…" she began. But how could she explain all she had lost to this stranger from a world so different from hers and Lamar's? His life was football and motorcycles and women picked up at honkytonks, not books and music and the wonderful quiet of this place. He would never understand how good her life had been and how empty it now was. Yet she wanted to make amends for what she had done to him.

"Here," she said, holding out the wad of bills.

"Oh, no you don't." Eddie took a step backward and raised his hands, warding her off. "I ain't falling for that. Just give me what I earned. One hundred and ninety-five dollars like you said. I don't want no more trouble."

"No, I mean it," she said, flapping the bills at him. "I want you to take it all."

He gave her a disgusted look. "And soon's I'm out of here you call the cops and say I stole it."

"What? I wouldn't do that. I'm not like that." She grabbed his hand and pressed the money into his palm. "Come on, take it. Please."

He let the bills sit on his palm for a moment. "It's lots more than I'm due." He shook his head. "You sure?"

She smiled and nodded. "Yes. You worked hard, out there in the sun."

He fanned the bills. "Nearly four hundred." He looked up at her, a quizzical yet pleased look on his face. "Well, if you want me to take it, I can sure use it."

She felt the tension flowing away and her breath came easier. "I hope you don't still think I'm a bad person." She nodded at the money. "That makes everything all right, doesn't it?"

Eddie stuck the money in the rear pocket of his jeans. "Yeah, well, I guess it wipes the dogshit off your shoe all right," he said, and then with a snuffling laugh added, "and the dogshit says thanks."

He walked out, grabbed his shirt from the porch railing and was down the steps.

She listened as his motorcycle stuttered into life and roared out of the driveway. They were both gone now, Eddie speeding over the hill to Madrono Valley where he wasn't treated like dogshit, and Lamar making his way to his new love, probably amused by his little spurt of jealousy. And here she was, alone with her soured revenge and this new wound she had inflicted on herself. She wandered around the cottage, gathering up ashtrays and ornaments, unplugging lamps, rolling up the scatter rugs. She'd be glad to be rid of this wretched place.

The Pioneer Women

IT'S THE FIRST DAY of the fall term, and Rachel stands at the lectern and looks out at the students—thirty or so young faces, handsome, relaxed, bronzed after a summer in the sun. Despite so many years of practice, she still feels the same old anxiety: will the class work? Will the students like her? So silly, these little moments of insecurity.

The air is hot from the mid-morning sun blasting through the closed windows, and Rachel seizes this as a chance to connect with the class. She pulls forward the collar of her blouse and fans her chest. "Will those sitting by the windows please open them, unless they're nailed shut." Grinning, the students on the aisle get up and tussle open the windows. The woman on the front row cannot open hers.

"Use your shoe and break the damn thing!" Rachel cries, and of course the class laughs. A short muscular man moves to the window and bangs so hard on the frame that the glass shivers. The window gives and he thrusts it up. The woman sits back down, her shoulders slumped forward in embarrassment. Rachel feels a twinge but shrugs it off: the class is now in a relaxed good mood.

Rachel distributes the syllabus, goes over the grading guidelines, and sails into backgrounds of American Romanticism. Just as she is connecting Rousseau and Wordsworth, a red-haired man interrupts, saying he had signed up for the course because it was supposed to be on American lit, not European. Rachel says, "American lit did not burst full-armed from the head of George Washington at Valley Forge." Now there's a thunder of laughter, and she's happy that the boy's laughter is loudest of all.

For the rest of the hour, Rachel talks and the students listen, and her anxiety slowly abates. After class the students file out. A few stop by the lectern, to check her out at closer range, to be checked out. A curly-headed man slips in the name of his uncle, a big-shot Hollywood director. Rachel nods and looks impressed. A blond woman says she memorized all of Wordsworth's "Hiawatha." Rachel lets the mistake go—she doesn't want to embarrass the woman.

The last student to leave is the woman who couldn't open the window. "That was a mean window, wasn't it?" Rachel says, a late apology. The woman nods. Drab clothes, timid slouch. "What's your name?" Rachel asks. This kind of inquiry is flattering to students and often breaks through shyness.

The woman says, "Elaine."

Rachel smiles. "No last name? Suppose I read in the newspaper that Elaine MacTavish won the lottery. I wouldn't know whether to ask for a loan, would I?" She has said the same kind of thing to other students. They like to be teased this way. They laugh and blush and say their full name.

The woman doesn't laugh, doesn't blush. She says, "Elaine Sherrill."

Rachel smiles. "That's a very pretty name." Elaine doesn't

respond. She is not to be charmed. Rachel begins to pack her books and her papers in her briefcase. "If there's nothing special I better get back to work."

The woman instantly starts for the door. Rachel wonders if she's hurt the woman's feelings again. "Come by my office sometime," she calls.

RACHEL stops by the Law School café and picks up a turkey sandwich and a carton of milk and goes to her office. She is working on the diaries of eight pioneer women, and she intends to have a rough draft of a book, her fourth, by summer. She spent the previous summer at various archives, photocopying diaries. This is an important project, and she guards her time jealously. Her friend Hennie has moved to Tucson, and she will not see him until Thanksgiving—he is as busy as she is, but with bats and DNA. This arrangement suits her: she is glad to devote herself to her wonderful pioneers.

She takes down one of the binders in which she keeps the diary photocopies, and for the next four hours, Mary MacTavish absorbs her. A bear had mauled Mary's husband, leaving her with 125 acres of wheat and five children. Mary's daughter Susan went to St. Louis to work and that was the last Mary heard of her. Her son Charles was killed at Bull Run. Colin and two younger sons remained at home. Colin married a neighbor's daughter and brought her back to live on the farm.

And then Rachel reads, "Colin decided we should plant 30 acres of corn," and then, "Colin bought 3 hens and a rooster." Colin decided. Colin bought. It is clear that after he married, Colin had assumed authority over the farm. Did sons always take over once they married? Was it customary for mothers to step aside? She'll check one of the other widows.

As she opens Winifred Stubblefield's diary, she hears a slight tapping on her door. It's awfully early in the term for students to drop by. "Come in," she calls impatiently.

The door slowly opens, and Elaine Sherrill enters in the halting, diffident manner of shy undergraduates, as though half-expecting to be thrown out without so much as a word. "Are you busy?" she asks.

Rachel motions to a chair alongside the desk. "I'm always happy when students drop by." She hadn't always found it easy to talk with students, to listen, but she had worked hard and had learned to do it, and she likes that they like talking with her. "Anything special on your mind?" she asks.

Elaine says, "You asked me to come by."

"So nothing special? Well, let's just get acquainted. Tell me about yourself. Family? Major? Ambition? Start with family."

In a muted, swallowed voice, Elaine launches into the story of her life: North Dakota, father an insurance adjuster, mother at home, two sisters, English major, hopes one day to get a Ph.D. A dull recitation of facts.

Rachel surreptitiously drags Winnie's diary closer but then she becomes aware that Elaine has stopped speaking and is watching the diary swimming slowly across the desk. Rachel pushes it back. "So what's your favorite kind of reading?" she asks.

Elaine says she reads short stories during the school term because a novel might interfere with her studying.

"Here, I bet you'd like this." Rachel motions Elaine to follow her to the bookcase. When students don't know when or how to leave, Rachel often offers to show them a particular book and guides them to the bookshelf. She puts the book in their hands. They glance at it and when they hand it back, she thanks them for dropping by and they leave. It is a little trick she learned when a teacher at Smith used it on her.

She goes to the bookcase and hesitates between Hawthorne's

Twice-Told Tales and a collection of Henry James stories. She decides James would be wasted on Elaine, and she hands the Hawthorne to her. Elaine actually begins to read the words. She could be there for hours. "Take it home and read it when you've finished your homework," Rachel says. "Thanks for dropping by."

Rachel feels good that she had thought to lend the book to Elaine. She knows how tough it is to be shy. But there is something off-putting about Elaine, not a typical student, not scrubbed and open-faced but uneasy and repressed. Still, a little friendly attention can make a difference with the shy ones.

Rachel returns to Winnie's diary. When Whistle dies, Winnie does not get another little dog because her son William says little dogs are useless on a farm. Here, too, the power has shifted. Now married, William makes the decision. Beneath patriarchy, does filiarchy flourish?

If this is borne out by her other widows, Betty and Clondie, she will have the important idea to hold her book together.

ELAINE Sherrill stations herself in the middle seat of the front row. This is disturbing, and so Rachel takes to lecturing from the side, perched on the window ledge, and makes only occasional visits to her notes on the lectern for a quotation or a specific number. She focuses on the back row where there's a couple who can't keep their hands off each other, a pretty girl who every day skates in on rollerblades and a broad-shouldered young man with greenish blond hair—probably on the water polo team soaking up the chlorine. Typical students, attractive, cheerful, confident.

When Rachel stays after class to talk with students, Elaine is always there. She stands apart and never asks a question.

IN the third week of the term, Elaine again comes to Rachel's office hours and returns *Twice-Told Tales*.

"Did you enjoy it?" Rachel asks.

"No."

This surprises Rachel. Most students would automatically say they liked a book a professor had recommended. "I'm sorry, I thought you'd like it."

"Why did you think that?" It's a serious question.

Turning the pages of the book, Rachel launches into a mini-lecture on the psychology of "The Minister's Black Veil" and "Wakefield" and "The Maypole of Merry Mount." After two or three minutes, she says, "Some readers find Hawthorne rather dull and gray, even Hawthorne himself, but I find him complex and profound." She closes the book and looks up at Elaine. Elaine is slumped over, hands massaging each other, hair lank against her sallow cheeks. Revulsion tightens like a fist around Rachel's groin. "I'm awfully sorry," she says, "but I have to make an important call now."

At the door, Elaine turns and smiles at Rachel. Her smile is sad, knowing, humiliated, as though she understands, even shares Rachel's feeling. Then she's gone.

A face surfaces from a distant memory. What was her name? RuthAnne? Yes. RuthAnne. She remembers that as RuthAnne passed in the junior high school corridor, the other girls sniggered and some held their noses in disgust and some whispered, "the Goon." Rachel remembers RuthAnne's raw, mottled face, her frizzy hair, and her long, hunched body, but most clearly she remembers her shamed, sickly smile. Like Elaine's.

With a sigh, Rachel opens Winifred's binder and flips through the pages. All of the sentences are declarative and none more than eight words. It's hard to say focused. She decides to take Ingrid Larsdotter's binder home for the evening, and tomorrow she'll go back to the widows.

After dinner she sits in her big leather armchair and looks over Ingrid's diary. Ingrid never married and lives with her two brothers and a sister-in-law on the Nebraska prairie. Rachel wishes she hadn't included Ingrid, but she's the only unmarried woman among her pioneers, and it would take time to find a different one. The pages drip bitterness and despair. Ingrid describes the smell of rancid sweat and manure and rotting wheat when her brothers "come tromping" to the table. She confides that she overheard her sister-in-law with the pouty lips refer to her as a "worm."

As she reads that, Rachel finds herself thinking of Elaine and the distaste she feels for her. Never before has she felt this revulsion for a student. She has had favorite students, of course, ones she found attractive, but she has prided herself on being fair and open to all. She tells herself that her reaction to Elaine is a moral failing that must be corrected. She is a teacher and Elaine is her student who deserves attention and a sensitive response, not contempt.

RACHEL is determined to overcome her revulsion. When she enters the classroom, she glances toward Elaine and greets her by name. She will not let herself move to the window, and when she throws out a question to the class, she looks to see if Elaine wants to answer it—she never does. The redheaded man always has his hand up. An attractive kid, good-looking, confident, smart and smart-alecky. Rachel likes him and likes teasing him. She always rolls her eyes and says, "You still yet and again?" And he grins, confident, loving the attention.

When the students gather at the lectern after the hour is over, Rachel makes a point of drawing Elaine into the group. The other students glance at Elaine, but no one speaks to her. They know. The worm. The goon.

IT'S the Wednesday before Thanksgiving. Hennie is flying in in early evening, and they will spend the holidays at the country house of friends in Napa. Before picking him up at the airport Rachel wants to get a bit further outlining her essay on the power struggle between the pioneer women and their newly married sons. After her class, she buys a sandwich in the basement cafeteria and goes to her office. She spends the next hours pouring over Clondie's diary, structuring her argument, identifying evidence, moving along.

And then there comes the rap on the door. She feels a clench of irritation, but she cheerily calls, "Come on in."

It's Elaine. Of course it's Elaine—no other student would be hanging around the campus so late the afternoon before a holiday. They'd be off skiing, having fun.

Elaine sits down, and to start the conversation—the better to get it over with—Rachel says she's sorry she assigned Melville's *Pierre: or, The Ambiguities,* that it's perhaps too dark and difficult for undergraduates. "Have you had any problem with it?" she asks Elaine.

"I'm not stupid," Elaine says.

Rachel is taken aback. "Well, I wasn't implying that. It's just that sometimes students have problems with Melville, not necessarily because they can't understand him but because they just don't see what's interesting. They don't see the flickers of humor, for instance. I bet you didn't think he was amusing, now did you?" She covers her acid tone by laughing lightly.

Elaine sucks in her breath with a little gasp and blinks her eyes rapidly. "No, I didn't." She begins to chew off the loose skin of her lips.

Rachel can't stand her repulsive presence another moment. "Sorry, but I have to finish something now," she says in a tense voice. Elaine picks up her backpack. At the door she turns and smiles that awful smile.

Once Elaine is gone, Rachel feels relief and guilt and a kind of sadness. With a sigh she goes back to the yellow tablet on which she was jotting notes. But the sun has dropped behind the clock tower and the office is growing dark. She will go home and take a little rest before picking up Hennie at the airport. Elaine's visit, she thinks, has drained all her energy.

A LIGHT rain falls early Thanksgiving morning and the country-side is fresh and fragrant. In late afternoon, Rachel and Hennie take a walk down the lane between the barren grape vines. Hennie tells her he has identified a new gene in his bats and hopes to isolate it in other mammals. She tells him about her women, the filiarchy, poor Ingrid Larsdotter.

And then she tells him about Elaine, how unattractive she is, how she sits like a toad in the middle of the front row, and about her own revulsion. "And of course she's hyper-sensitive. You know how some unattractive people can be all exposed nerves, finding a slight in every eye blink?" Rachel feels a pang of remorse. "Well, but she just wants a mentor or something." She shrugs. "A lot of students are looking for mentors. I used to hang around my professors when I was at Smith." She laughs ruefully. "I was a real pest."

"I wish you hung around me more," says Hennie, pulling her to him and kissing her on the cheek. "The love of my life." They both laugh. Hennie's work is the love of his life, as her work is hers. Both had failed at marriage. In graduate school, she had found Mick—her first lover and as lonely as she had been—but while she had worked so hard to finish her degree and then as an assistant professor and Mick sold software, they had grown apart until finally they had hated each other. She had changed, he said, and she had said, Thank God for that. After the divorce, Mick had married and soon had two sons. She was glad: nothing to regret. She feels lucky to have worked it out with Hennie so that both are content.

IT'S December and only one week remains in the term. Rachel re-minds the students that their papers are due at the last class and that the final will be the following Thursday. "Having done the reading could help. Also having stayed awake in class." And of course the students laugh. "If you have any questions, drop by my office."

All afternoon they drop by, a few to discuss the exam, a few to get an extension on their essay, a few still looking for an essay topic. The redheaded man comes in. He has thirty major ideas for a fifteen-page paper. For the next ten minutes they narrow his project, teasing each other, laughing.

When he leaves, it's Elaine's turn.

"If you want an extension," Rachel says, "you can have until the day of the final without a penalty."

Elaine looks insulted. "I don't need an extension."

"Good. So what can I do for you?" Rachel impatiently drums her fingers against her knee under the desk. And then get out, she thinks.

"I wanted to know if it's all right to write my paper on your idea,"

"Treatment is everything. What idea?"

"Melville's humor. You said you thought he was humorous," Elaine says.

"Did I say that?" Rachel doesn't remember saying anything about Melville to Elaine. "Well, I certainly didn't mean humorous like, say, Mark Twain. But Melville's a good choice." When Elaine doesn't respond, Rachel begins to talk about her fondness for Melville, his depth, his contrariness, and, okay, his humor. Then she stands up. "Here let me show you this great picture of him."

"Why don't you just tell me to leave?" Elaine grabs her backpack and heads for the door.

"Now just a minute," Rachel begins, but she sees that terrible smile, and then Elaine is gone.

RuthAnne. That smile. Rachel thinks of the last time she had spoken to RuthAnne. RuthAnne had caught up with her after school and clutched her arm and said, "I've got cigarettes. Come home with me and we can smoke. It was fun last week, wasn't it?"

Rachel had seen the other girls watching, judging, smirking, and she had felt herself flushing and almost weeping. "I won't go home with you, I hate you," she had said and had run off.

After that Rachel had spent her afternoons studying in the musty library, hearing the shouts and squeals from the grassy field where the students gathered. Then evenings of algebra and geography and weekends reading Austen, imagining that she was Elizabeth Bennet.

She never spoke to RuthAnne again.

Guilt, Rachel thinks. Somehow Elaine has dug up the whole RuthAnne thing. Not that Elaine looks anything like RuthAnne. Small and rather delicate, not raw-boned like RuthAnne. A smudgy, darkish complexion, not blotchy red. And she's smart, which no one ever accused RuthAnne of being. Strange that a guilt can last half a century and then transfer to someone else. She wishes she had never met Elaine.

ELAINE does very well on the exam, answers all the factual questions correctly, and shows real insight and understanding on the essay questions—the best exam in the class. Her paper on Melville's humor, though overloaded with the opinions of critics, is thoughtful and carefully written and even shows smidgens of buried humor, like Melville's. Rachel is glad to give Elaine an A+ for the course. She knows Elaine will be thrilled, as she herself had been when she received an A+. All's well that ends well. Rachel has never been happier to see the end of the term, the last of a student.

CHRISTMAS comes and with it Hennie. He says his lab is doing something spectacular and he can only stay three days. One evening after Hennie leaves, she goes to the movies with her bachelor friend Guy who is a Medievalist, on another has dinner with another Americanist and her new husband, briefly attends a New Year's Eve party at a neighbor's, and spends the rest of the time on her pioneer women.

When she finishes outlining the article on the widows and their sons, she sets it aside to let it mellow and turns to her other women. Nina Casper lives alone in the backwoods of the Appalachian Mountains in North Carolina. Leah Stein is married to a peddler gone from home weeks at a time. Lizzie Comstock's husband is a circuit preacher. Rachel is very happy working. She likes the company of these brave women.

ON the third day of the new term, as Rachel sits at her desk looking through Leah's diary, she hears a tap on the door and calls Come in, and there's Elaine, drenched from the sudden rain. Rachel had not thought about Elaine once during the holidays, but now it all storms back: the tedious encounters, her revulsion, RuthAnne.

Rachel motions Elaine to the chair by the desk. "Come to complain about getting an A+?" she asks with a laugh.

"I wanted to ask your advice," Elaine says, "on how to become a professor." She looks down at her hands, then up again, a shy smile playing on her lips. "I want to know how I can get from where I sit to where you sit."

Sit where she sits? Other students have asked similar questions, seeking advice on what courses to take, where to apply for graduate work. Rachel has sometimes encouraged them, sometimes not. She will not encourage Elaine. Elaine just doesn't have what it takes.

Rachel puts on a thoughtful expression and says, "Well, your paper showed you could do the research, and you did very well on the exam. But I'm not sure I'd recommend it as a profession. It's not the cushy job it may seem—it's hard work. There were years when I thought about nothing but work morning, noon, and night."

Elaine says, "I'm happiest when I'm studying and working."

"Well, so was I, but of course it's not just the work." It's impossible to picture Elaine holding office hours or lecturing to a class of bright, critical students. They'd be trampling each other to get out the door. "It takes other things."

Elaine leans forward. "But can't I learn those other things?"

Never, Rachel thinks. Before she can figure out how to discourage Elaine without being cruel, there's a tapping on the door and the department chair sticks his head into the room. He smiles apologetically and says, "Sorry. Didn't mean to interrupt." He's carrying his briefcase and umbrella, ready to go home, a plump, easygoing, good-natured man. Rachel is always happy to see him, never more than now.

"Come on in," she says. "We're finished."

Elaine stands up. At the door she smiles the terrible complicit smile, as though she and Rachel had forged a bond.

The department chair merely wants to ask Rachel to serve on the graduate studies committee. How could she refuse him when he has saved her from such an unpleasant moment and perhaps from saying or doing something she would regret. For a few minutes they chat about the department and the university and then the chair leaves.

Rachel feels unsettled and restless, and she calls Guy, and asks him if he's ever had an Elaine Sherrill in his class, and Guy laughs and says he only remembers the boys. "She giving you grief?"

Rachel's feelings of revulsion and guilt are too personal, too unprofessional, to share even with Guy. "She wrote a really good paper in my class last quarter, and I just wondered if she was one of our Honors students." Because that's so weak, she quickly adds, "Actually, I was calling to see if you're too busy with the boys to go to the movies. I need a break."

They arrange to go to the new Spanish film.

When Rachel hears the rain beating on the roof, she goes to the window and braces her hands on the ledge and presses her forehead against the cold pane. It had rained almost continuously the winter she and her parents had moved to California. Every day she had sloshed through the puddles and arrived at the junior high school drenched, her sneakers oozing water, her hair plastered to her cheeks, her moist wool clothes smelling like wet dog. She had felt utterly alone. And then along came RuthAnne to befriend her. The other girls—giggling, chirping, whispering to each other—looked at them thinking, Two of a kind, two goons. Rachel had not been able to bear that. She remembers as though she had just read it the plaintive, begging note RuthAnne had written: Please be my friend again. She shakes her head at the irony. It's too many years too late to make amends.

IT is still raining the next day. Rain stands ankle-deep in declivities on the pathways and leaves greasy tracks down the office windows. After a dull lecture in which Rachel fails to elicit from the students even a pretended interest in Emerson, she picks her way through the rain, buys her sandwich and milk, and goes back to her office.

She decides to work on Clondie and flips through Clondie's binder, looking for a good quotation to get her going. She reads once more about Clondie's silent son, Lillard, and her silly daughter-in-law who pinches color into her cheeks when the preacher calls. Clondie reports this and everything else in a dull and plaintive tone. Clondie is like Elaine, repressed, meager, miserable. Another boring choice she had made, like Ingrid.

Rachel goes to the bookshelf and runs her fingers over the backs of the binders, choosing a different one. But all the women remind her of Elaine. Nina's smothered fury. Leah's desperate loneliness. Winifred's dullness. Even Mary's useless intelligence. Elaine has infected the project. She has contaminated the pioneer women.

Rachel wants to tell Hennie how discouraged she is, but when she calls Tucson, he is in neither his office nor his apartment. Where could he be? Has he found someone else, as Mick had? Hennie is always commenting on young women, this one breasty, that one with great legs, another with a gorgeous youthful face. Rachel always laughs, taking it as a joke. But she knows she's not attractive that way, has never been. It was only a matter of time when he would move on. Anyway, she thinks, he is in love with his work, and she was never more than a convenience for him. He has probably found a more attractive convenience.

The tower clock bongs six times, and Rachel listens to the empty building around her. She thinks of her colleagues snug in their homes, sipping martinis in front of a roaring fire, the department head with his pretty wife perched on the arm of his chair, ruffling his few remaining strands of hair, the Americanist and her husband deep in intimate talk. Even her friend Guy is somewhere with someone.

She looks up at the diaries and shakes her head. The project is dead. The diaries are too dull, too dreary. She can't imagine why she ever found the miserable women appealing. What she needs is a new project.

Hawthorne? Emerson? Stowe? James? Yes, Henry James. She's had some interesting ideas about various women in his life, Minnie and Constance and Alice and Henry's mother. Attractive, clever women, not like the pioneers. They would make an exciting book.

She decides to go home, to have a glass of wine and spend the evening steeping herself in *The Portrait of a Lady*. Tomorrow she'll start on the background reading and thinking. Maybe that will break her awful gloom.

She pulls on her raincoat and opens the door, and there's Elaine sitting on the corridor bench where students wait their turn.

"Hello," Elaine says, standing. Raincoat dripping water, stringy hair lank along her cheeks, moist hands gripping the backpack.

Rachel feels the kick of revulsion. "Kind of late for office hours," she says in a deliberately hostile voice.

"I didn't want to interrupt your work."

You've already done that, Rachel wants to say. You've ruined it. "I'm on my way out. Try me next week."

"Just for a minute," Elaine says. "I want to ask you something—it won't take long and then I'll never bother you again."

Anything to finally be rid of this pariah. Rachel motions Elaine toward the usual chair and sits down without bothering to remove her raincoat. She won't let this take long. She leans back and locks her hands behind her head, hardly controlling her distaste. "So what's on your mind?"

"The same thing as yesterday. Remember I asked you how I could become what you are?" She pauses. "Can you talk to me now?"

Rachel laughs dismissively. "Well, work hard, keep your nose clean. That's about all I can tell you."

Elaine's face is serious, questioning. "You don't like me, do you?" she says.

"What?" Rachel drops forward and slaps the arms of her chair. She could never have anticipated this and isn't sure how to react. "Look, you're a student, I'm a professor," she says, throwing her hands up to show how exasperated she is. "I'm not in the habit of getting emotionally involved with students so that I like or dislike them. What's your problem anyway?"

"My problem?" Elaine's eyes fill. "I'm miserable, I hate what I am, and I thought you would understand."

"Well, I'm sorry you're not happy," Rachel says, "but I don't know what that has to do with me. I'm just a teacher, not a psychiatrist."

"But weren't you unhappy when you were my age?"

"Isn't everyone?"

"No," Elaine says. "Those girls and boys, no, they're not miserable. Maybe anxious about the future, maybe alone for a short while, but not miserable. They know they'll recover. But you were, weren't you?"

Rachel doesn't like being questioned this way, but she rolls her eyes. "Of course I was. Lots of the time. Most of the time." She laughs an ironic little laugh. "All of the time?"

"I knew that," Elaine says, leaning forward. "But you overcame it. How? What did you do to become..." She pauses. "...what you are now? I want to change. I don't want to be dull and gray and miserable and sometimes I just don't want to be alive. Tell me what I can do, what you did. Please help me."

Rachel wants to end this terrible encounter, to get this pitiful woman out of her office, out of her life. "I don't know why you'd come to me. I can't help you," she says. "No one can."

She puts her hands on the desk, ready to push herself up. But as she sees her words register on Elaine's face, the past that she had thought buried erupts, and what she sees is not RuthAnne but herself. She knows exactly what Elaine is feeling—the fear, the fury, the loneliness, the self-loathing. Oh, she knows all this very well indeed. The feeling of despair is there all the time, deeply buried now, but ready to leap out. But it doesn't have to, not if you don't let it. She reaches across the corner of the desk and puts her hand over Elaine's where it grips her backpack.

"What I mean is, it's up to you. You can be who you want to be. It's not impossible. You can overcome everything. I did it. I was a goon and I overcame it. So can you." She tightens her grip on Elaine's hand and nods insistently. "You're smart, just as I was, and you'll learn, just as I did. I promise you you'll be okay. Don't give up. That's how you do it. You don't give up. Promise me you won't give up."

When Rachel releases her hand, Elaine says, "I won't. Thank you." She stands up and hoists her backpack onto her shoulder and heads for the door.

Rachel calls, "Come back and let's talk again." As she watches the door close, she thinks, It's true, Elaine won't always be a goon. She'll overcome it. Slowly the goon will disappear. I did it. She can do it.

After a moment, Rachel goes over to the diaries. She feels foolish that she had ever thought of deserting these terrific women for pampered Bostonians who had so little to overcome. Mary Mac-Tavish is so much more than just the mother of a domineering son—she had schooled the neighbor children and had sent her youngest son off to the new land-grant college even though Colin had wanted him to stay on the farm. And Winnie—her sentences are dull, yes, but she had raised her three children alone in a cold and lonely place and managed to record it all. And the others, too, courageous women who had created a new world for themselves, who had made something out of the little they were given, just as she had done, just as Elaine will.

Rachel thinks of Hennie. He was probably driving home when she called. She had been silly to worry, inventing trouble. He's busy, just as she is. When she gets home she'll call him and arrange for a weekend, perhaps in La Jolla.

She puts Clondie and Betty in her briefcase and steps out into the misty night. One of the stray campus cats crouches on a windowsill. In the distance, a young man and a young woman astride their bicycles are laughing and talking. Rachel sets out across the Quad. She's eager to spend the evening with her wonderful pioneer women.

Squaring the Circle

WE WERE WIDOWS when we moved into Ridgeside Retirement Residence. We all had children who were to different degrees affectionate and available, but we were of the generation proud not to be dependent on them. Let them lead their life unfettered by old folks, we said, wishing our life had been unfettered by old folks. We set up special occasions to see them and our grandchildren, taking them to restaurants they wouldn't spend the money to go to on their own or renting a vacation house at Sea Ranch or Lake Tahoe.

And then we found each other. After that, though we sometimes groused that we had slipped between the cracks of our children's lives, we didn't really mind. Our gang at Triple R had become our real life. We always had a project, such as attending a rally for the Democratic senatorial hopeful or a weekend visiting all the museums in LA. We often read plays together, and once we went to a town on the Feather River to buy hand-embroidered blouses from an Indian tribe—none of us ever wore the blouses for fear we'd see our mirror image coming down the hall, but we had all enjoyed the visit.

There were other gangs at Triple R. The gang we called the Bar Flies met in the bar for drinks almost every night, and sometimes got tipsy and danced along the corridors, singing old songs. The Jockos played golf at the nearby country club and perfected their putting on Triple R's practice green, all looking hale and hardy except for their skin, leathered by too many California suns. The Card Sharks met every afternoon to play bridge, and through the evening we could hear them rehashing the hands they had played, often lamenting that a slam could have been made if only. The Weight Watchers enrolled in the exercise classes and spent hours walking in twos and threes around the grounds, hoping to work off the pounds with a minimum of pain. A few of the residents were Floaters and moved from one group to another, never quite committing—the few widowers who came to Triple R were Floaters until they hooked up with a widow from another group and became whatever that person was. And there were the Lone Rangers, not really a gang but individuals who silently ate their meals at the communal table and then rushed back to their lonely apartments to do whatever Lone Rangers do.

The other groups had their nicknames for us, of course. As we walked toward the dining room, some one might call out in a teasing voice, What are the Cracked Eggheads hatching now? or Hide, here come the Culture Vultures, or some other friendly insult. We didn't mind being ribbed—we were happy to have our gang.

None of us ever actually said so, but Martha was our leader. At sixty-nine she was the youngest though not by much, and full of energy and ideas. After her three children had grown up, she had gone to work for a non-profit and for fifteen years was its head. One of those odd yet fairly common things happened: the year she retired her husband died as though he had just been hanging on until she had time to take over. After she had settled his affairs and sold her house, she moved into Triple R, tired, she said, of looking after the garage, the garden, the roof, the basement, and everything in between all by herself. We had laughed because we had all been there and were glad now to be at Triple R.

AND then the General came along. Walter Latimer was his name, but we always thought of him as "the General," even after he had been among us a while. He moved into Triple R on a Friday and by the traditional Sunday brunch, all four hundred and sixty residents were aware of him. We knew he had been a Major General in Kuwait in '91 for the first Iraq war. After he retired, he and his wife had moved to Santa Fe, and when she died he came to the Bay Area and Triple R, to be closer to his daughter in San Francisco. Although he had exchanged his army uniform for the usual blue blazer, he had retained his military bearing, his backbone perpendicular and his shoulders parallel. He wore his thick gray hair in an old-fashioned brush cut and clipped his moustache close and neat, and of course you could see your reflection in his black shoes.

That first week whenever the General marched through the dining room, heads rose and faces turned toward him with broad smiles. Even if they were nearing eighty and alone for twenty years, many of the Triple R widows had held onto their romantic aspirations and always kept their eye out, not exactly expecting anything, but just in case. The General seemed oblivious to all the interest he excited. He took his long strides straight through the room as though on military parade. Ellie, who had a keener eye than the rest of us, said one of the Bar Flies would snag him within a week. And with a disparaging laugh, Jeannette, our divorcée, said no one would want him.

Our first real contact with him occurred when we were in the library off the main lobby, where we had met to read Chekhov's

Three Sisters. Before we got started, we were gossiping about the General and just as Rena said, "He'd probably call reveille at six A.M.," speak of the devil and there he was, passing in the hall just outside the room. We grinned and giggled a little bit at the coincidence, and then we started our reading, deepening our voices to read the male roles and prissing a bit when we played the women we didn't like. Instead of moving on as any decent person would, the General came to stand right in the doorway, his arms crossed as though he were judging a military exercise.

As Martha was reading the first speech of Baron Tuzenbakh, the General stepped into the room and leaned over her shoulder. "Give his voice some heft," he barked, "Tuzenbakh's a soldier, not a schoolmarm."

Ruth said in her quiet voice, "Tuzenbakh isn't a typical soldier."

The General snuffled a derisive laugh. "Typical soldier enough to put his honor above his life."

That is just what Tuzenbakh does—allows himself to be pointlessly killed in a duel rather than be thought a coward. To be truthful, we were less surprised that the General dared interfere—after all we couldn't expect a General to be anything but overbearing—than that he actually knew Chekhov well enough to have an opinion about Baron Tuzenbakh. Our notions about the army did not come tumbling down—our scorn for militarism was too deeply embedded for that—but it was obvious that we were shaken. We looked around at each other, wondering if we had been completely misreading the play.

But Martha was having none of it. "You read Chekhov in your way," she said in her quiet voice, "and we'll read him in his way."

Without another word, the General turned smartly on his heels and departed. We looked at Martha, marveling at her poise, her cleverness. "You certainly shut him up," Rena said, chortling. "'In his way' was wonderful."

"I'm afraid it wasn't original," Martha said sheepishly. "I read something like that somewhere."

"Never apologize, never explain," Gertie said. "You were great."

Ellie said, "What an insufferable fool."

Jeannette said, "The typical conceited male."

Ruth said, "You can be a soldier without being insensitive."

Carla said, "A perfect symbol of the arrogant military. All he needs is a swagger stick flicking against his thigh."

Once we thought we had racked him up pretty well, we went back to the play and picked up where we had stopped. But after a few minutes we realized the General had ruined our mood. Martha even said that perhaps she should give Tuzenbakh a bit more backbone—not, she quickly added, because he was a military man but because Irina wouldn't want to marry a weakling.

After just a few more pages, we knew we had lost the spirit, and since it was dinnertime we decided to give it up and start from the beginning when we met again.

The next day Rena and Jeannette had plans to go to the de Young to see the Chinese calligraphy exhibit, and then came the weekend. So we didn't meet again until the next Tuesday afternoon. When Martha came in the room, she looked red-nosed and rheumy-eyed, and she said she had caught a cold, perhaps from one of her grandchildren over the weekend, and didn't want to spread whatever it was she had.

Once she had left, we closed the door, in case the General came marching by. Jeannette agreed to be Tuzenbakh as well as Olga, and so we began the reading. After a few pages we all knew it wasn't going well, that it just wasn't right without Martha. Still, we plowed on in a desultory way until Tuzenbakh is killed and the soldiers say goodbye and the sisters cry and we all felt very sad.

We didn't meet as a group for a week, though most of us had dinner together and a few went to a dreadful play at the University and Carla and Gertie did some early Christmas shopping at a craft fair in San Francisco.

Then Martha said she felt better and we should get going on something, and we set up a meeting.

As several of us were walking through the lobby toward the meeting room, we looked out the large window that opens onto the rose garden. Rena said, "Isn't that Martha?" and Ellie said, "Isn't that the General?" Martha was sitting on the stone bench looking up, and the General was standing with one foot on the bench, elbow on knee, and chin on hand, looking down. "I bet he's giving her hell," Rena said, and Jeannette said, "And I hope she's giving him the dregs of her cold," and we all laughed.

When we told Martha we had seen her in the garden being fussed at by the General, she said, "He wasn't fussing. He was explaining."

"How to do the play, the arrogant bastard," Jeannette said.

"No, no," Martha said. "Explaining why he interfered. In the eighties he was the military attaché in Moscow and saw a Russian production of *Three Sisters*. Apparently the Russians played it with an edge."

"He sees the play once and he thinks he's Chaliapin," Ellie said.

"He's not quite that arrogant," Martha said with a laugh. "Poor guy just got carried away. Because he loves the play."

"Probably hasn't seen another one since," Rena said.

"That's what's so sad," Martha said. "He hasn't had much opportunity for things like that."

We were surprised that Martha had so easily accepted the General's explanation. Most of us wouldn't forgive so easily—we had spent too much of our married years accepting male excuses for bad behavior. We probably wouldn't have admitted it aloud, but not having to do that anymore was one of the small joys of widowhood.

Carla said. "Well, old soldiers may not die, but let's just let that one fade away." We laughed at that and began to discuss what we would read next. Rena suggested Albee's *Who's Afraid of Virginia Woolf* but Jeannette vetoed that because it reminded her too much of her own marriage. Ellie thought something new from Broadway, but Rena said if we hadn't seen or read it, we couldn't know whether it was worth our while.

"How about a Shakespeare?" Martha said. "Haven't ever done one of those."

Ruth then suggested *Romeo and Juliet* and Jeanette thought *Macbeth* would be fun. Ellie said both of those were too heavy, so what about *As You Like It?* After ten minutes or so debating the pros and cons of tragedies and comedies, Martha said, "Maybe something in the middle? like *Measure for Measure?*" and so that's what we decided to read. We would all study the play over the weekend and then meet to figure out who would take which role.

AFTER we had done our homework, we gathered late Monday afternoon in our usual room off the lobby. Because she had gone to the mixer Triple R put on, Martha wasn't there when the rest of us arrived. That was a little unusual, but as we waited Gertie said we weren't stapled together at the hip. Occasionally one or another of us went to the mixer, if for no other reason, Ellie said, than at least we got to drink some of the booze we had to pay for whether we drank it or not.

When Martha arrived, she looked a tad flushed and a little nervous. We knew she wasn't drunk—she always nursed one drink through a whole evening. Ruth suggested maybe she should go back to bed and nurse that cold a bit more. But Martha said the party room had just been a little too warm.

We turned to *Measure for Measure.* Gertie said she'd like to read a woman's part since she had had two male parts in *Three*

Sisters, and Jeannette said she wouldn't mind reading a male role if she could be the executioner, and after we had laughed at that, Rena said she would play a male if she could be the young and handsome Claudio.

"Who's going to be the Duke?" Carla asked.

And that's when Martha said, "Since there are so many characters, it might get too confusing if it's just us reading all the parts. What if we invited some of the other Triple Rs to join in? Just this one time. Maybe one of the men could play the Duke?"

"Ha!" Carla said, "Imagine one of the Bar Flies as the Duke."

"Or imagine one of the Jockos," Rena said.

Martha shrugged. "Not a Bar Fly or a Jocko." She paused. "Maybe the General. He has the bearing and the voice for it."

We didn't exactly reel back, but we were all definitely shocked. "That oaf," Rena said, and Gertie said, "Over my dead body."

Martha raised her hands as though warding off an attack. "Never mind. It was just a thought."

"Maybe Shakespeare is too ambitious," Ruth said in her quiet way. "Perhaps we should try something a bit simpler? What do you think, Martha?"

Martha wasn't exactly examining her fingernails, but she had definitely disengaged. "Oh, I made my suggestion," she said. "Now it's someone else's turn."

Martha had never shown the slightest petulance before, and we decided she was obviously still sick. To take the pressure off her, we agreed that each of us would come up with a suggestion for a different play by the next time we met. As we walked back to our apartments, Carla said, "When Martha acts like that, you know she's really sick."

"She's not sick," Jeannette said. "It's the General."

We thought that was just Jeannette being a bit snide. But then she told us that she had twice in the past three days seen Martha and the General together, one afternoon drinking tall glasses of lemonade down in the bar and another time in the shopping center at Nordstrom's necktie department. And then it seemed that over the past few days we had all had our "sightings," as Rena put it: the two of them on the putting green, at Baskin-Robbins, standing in line at a movie, once in a downtown Burmese restaurant.

"Well," Rena said, "she certainly hasn't been coming to lunch or dinner with any of us." Not that we ate our meals together all the time. Jeannette, for instance, preferred lunch in her apartment eating the cottage cheese and canned pear that helped her control her weight, Carla often spent a day at the shopping center, and Ellie went out to dinner with old friends from earlier times.

Rena said she didn't keep track of who was or wasn't present for meals but without Martha the dining room certainly wasn't as pleasant as it had once been.

And then we wondered why we had not discussed Martha's absence. Was it, Ruth suggested, a sense of privacy we protected for ourselves and wouldn't violate in others? It's her business, isn't it? We all nodded and tacitly agreed that it was indeed Martha's business and we wouldn't discuss it.

When we met next to decide on the new play, Martha mentioned it to us. "I don't know whether you've noticed," she said, "but I haven't been around as much as usual."

"Oh, we noticed all right," Jeannette said.

Martha said, "It's because I've been seeing Walter."

Ellie immediately said, "What exactly does 'seeing' mean in this context?"

We all knew Ellie had a vulgar streak, and so we rushed right past her. "Well, we've missed you," Rena said.

"And we're glad to see you," Ruth said.

But Carla wouldn't leave it there. "That explains why you wanted to open the play to Triple R," she said.

"No, no, not at all," Martha dismissed that with a wave. "Though I did—do—think we're getting a tad stale, ingrown. But I'm okay if the rest of you want to keep our gang closed. So what're we doing next?"

That was all the conversation we had about Martha and the General. As Ruth had made clear, we weren't about to invade each other's privacy, except Ellie's one little mistake. Even later and in private, none of us ever mentioned *seeing* him. Of course we were curious and had to wonder, but we were old enough to keep our imaginings under control.

We began to discuss our next reading. Ellie suggested *Private Lives* and Ruth suggested *Winterset* and then Jeannette said, "How about Clare Booth Luce's old play, *The Women*. It doesn't have a single male character."

We snuck glances at Martha to see how she would take that, but she just shrugged and said, "Since we can't seem to settle, let's think about it some more and decide next week."

MARTHA didn't come to lunch or dinner during the week, and when one of us arranged an outing, to a concert in San Francisco one evening and a lecture over at the University another, and invited her, she was sorry but had other plans. And those plans were always with the General. We saw them eating together, going on walks around the premises, getting in the General's car for a jaunt here or there. After all the years of widowhood when she had not at all been one of those avid old women on the prowl for anything in pants but had been quite content with being a widow among women, here she was, in the twilight of her life with what Gertie persisted in calling a boyfriend.

And then she didn't even show up for our next meeting, when we were to settle on the next play. We pretended nothing was different but of course everything was. Still, as the General might have said, we soldiered on, making suggestions for what we should try next.

Ellie said, "You didn't like my suggestion of *Private Lives*, but how about *Blithe Spirit*? That would be fun."

Rena said, "It's so trivial—it would be a waste of time."

Ruth said, "I was thinking, how about Chekhov's *The Cherry Orchard*?"

Carla said, "We should never try Chekhov again, after that awful *Three Sisters*."

One by one we dismissed each other's ideas with impatient sighs and a flap of the hand. And then Jeannette said, "I still think *The Women* would be great."

Rena whipped around to face her. "Harping on that is what drove Martha away."

"Wait just a second," Jeannette said, her face flaming.

Gertie in her airy way said, "Oh, come on, Jeannette, if the shoe fits…"

Ellie turned on Gertie and said, "Must you always speak in clichés?"

We pushed back our chairs, gathered up our belongings, and left the room, furious with each other and ashamed of ourselves. Were we envious that Martha had found the General and we had not? Maybe, but most of us had long since given up any expectation that our life could take a romantic turn and in all sincerity would not have wanted that turn and its inevitable complication.

Were we simply jealous of the General because we had lost Martha to him, just as we had been jealous as girls when some stupid boy picked off our best friend? Yet we would not admit how distressed we were. We said it was only the inevitable order of nature, just as when the peacock spreads his fancy tail feathers before the peahen and the rest of the covey scatters.

———

SO we scattered. Although two or three of us occasionally went to a play or concert or ate together, we were no longer a gang. We had lost the center of our circle and the group fell apart. Ellie became a Bar Fly and one evening the night manager had to put her to bed, and for three days she stayed out of sight. Jeannette decided to lose twenty-five pounds, and every morning she exercised with the Weight Watchers and every evening emptied the breadbasket. Rena took up golf again and spent long hours alone on the putting green, bent over, trying to figure out which way the grass grew. Gertie began playing gin rummy with whoever happened into the card room, and occasionally she was asked to fill in at the bridge table. Like a butterfly in a high wind Carla seemed unable to land and became a Floater. Ruth took her meals up to her room, reverting to her natural state of Lone Ranger.

ABOUT seven months after our gang broke up, the General died. He and Martha had been attending a mixer when he dropped his glass of wine on the carpet, gave out a muted groan, and crumbled to the floor. Martha dropped to her knees and rubbed his hands between hers, beseeching him to be all right. But he died almost instantly. The night manager took charge and hurried the General's body out the back door of Triple R, and the desk clerk quickly escorted Martha up the service elevator to her apartment.

Apparently the General had never been ill a day in his life, except once when he broke his elbow falling from a horse during a steeplechase. We all thought he would have made a very demanding patient, and that all in all a one-minute heart attack was not a bad way for such a man to go. Or, really, anyone.

FOR the first week or so after the General's death, Martha did not venture out of her apartment. She and the General had been such a tight twosome that they had not made couple-friends, and of course Martha' s children didn't take the romance seriously and hardly showed up after the first day. Although we were still smarting a little, we swallowed our pride and went up to her apartment. As we embraced her, we silently forgave her for deserting us and ourselves for deserting each other. The next day Ellie brought a bottle of dry sherry and Jeannette a wheel of Brie and crackers and Carla an armload of flowers. Rena and Gertie took turns making sure the staff prepared Martha a hot dinner each night, and Ruth collected the mail from Martha's mailbox.

After almost two weeks, Martha did what we would expect her to do. She had her hair done in the basement beauty salon, put on her makeup, donned a beautiful lavender dress, and came forth to meet the world as it would be.

Jeannette arranged for the seven of us to sit together at the large round table in the window. Ellie ordered a special wine, and Carla made sure the flower arrangement matched the daffodils and iris just beginning to bloom in the garden. Martha was the last to appear, her lightly colored hair swept back, her shoulders as squared as the General's had ever been.

She sat down, unfolded her napkin across her lap, and looked at each of us, one by one, smiling, as though reminding herself of how much we meant to her. And then she said, "Shall we try *The Cherry Orchard* again?" Beaming with pleasure we said what a marvelous idea that was. And we felt safe again.

Two's Company

ROSA PERDIDO WAS four feet eleven inches of muscle and energy, every erg packed with prickle. Virginia Blankenship was six slender feet of controlled good manners. One dark, the other fair. One poor, the other well off. One an immigrant from Manila, the other not quite back to the Mayflower but close. Of an age, which was a year or so over sixty. For eleven months, they had met every Tuesday in the Blankenships' seven-room flat on the Upper East Side of Manhattan, where Rosa did the cleaning and the laundry and Virginia wrote children's books.

Rosa admired Mrs. B, as she called Virginia. The cashmere sweaters, the well-kept nails, the brownstone full of expensive textures and elegant antiques, the husband who wore dark suits and silk neckties and spoke in a soft voice. And she was proud of working for a writer, a real writer. Shortly after Rosa had begun working for the Blankenships, Mrs. B had given her a copy of *The Crocodile's Dinner Party* signed "To my friend Rosa." On her way home to Brooklyn, Rosa often stopped in at Barnes and Noble in Grand

Central to make sure the book was prominently displayed in the Children's Books section and to tell the clerk that Virginia Blankenship was her very good friend. At these moments Rosa loved Mrs. B.

But something would happen between them, and then the woman's very existence brought bile to Rosa's mouth and rage to her heart. Leaving the room before Rosa had finished her story. Explaining how to run the new vacuum cleaner or how to apply for citizenship, things Rosa knew better than Mrs. B did. And sometimes Mrs. B spoke with irritation when Rosa was trying to do her work. Just a stupid rich woman.

Rosa was sure that she was smarter than Mrs. B and knew things Mrs. B had never even heard of and done things Mrs. B would shudder to know and lived in places that would frighten Mrs. B bald-headed. If she had had half Mrs. B's chances, she would have done much better than Mrs. B ever could. She would have a grander apartment than Mrs. B's, not decorated in pale, washed-out colors but in rich reds and blues. She would have written a large, important book, a book for grown-ups, not a teeny tiny book for kids who couldn't even read them. And she wouldn't be married to a wimp like Mr. B but to someone bold and confident—at least that son-of-a-bitch Antonio hadn't been a sissy with a puny voice and soft useless hands.

Virginia never came close to "loving" Rosa, but she did admire her gritty determination. She admired the fact that Rosa had taken classes at night school and spoke an absolutely perfect English, that Rosa took pains with her appearance and came to work decked out in stylish designer clothing that she proudly said she bought for a song at a nearly-new shop just off Madison, that she took pride in doing a good job, dreary as the work was, and left the apartment gleaming. And she was absolutely honest. Virginia never had a moment's doubt of that. Rosa was too proud to steal.

But Virginia found Rosa's very presence intrusive and annoying. From the moment Rosa arrived, the air seemed to swell with her bustling energy, chairs scraping, doors slamming, pots and pans clanging. Worst of all was Rosa's proud voice telling endless stories of her life. Whenever she saw Virginia, even just passing in the hallway, she seized the moment to launch into one of her tales, how she had overcome the misery of her childhood, how she had defeated the "scum" she encountered on the subway, and, more cheerfully, how she had taken a fancy to a little Puerto Rican boy. It was as if part of Rosa's pay was access to Virginia's ear. Even when Virginia managed to escape to her workroom, Rosa soon brought in her bucket of cloths and sponges, saying, "Okay if I clean in here?" as though Virginia were just playing with the crayons, like a child. When Virginia had complained to Lawrence about Rosa, he had blithely answered, Just tell her to come back later. He could be incredibly dense. She couldn't possibly say, Go clean the toilets while I diddle with these crayons. It was unbearable. She'd have to let Rosa go, give her two weeks' pay and send her on her way. But not yet. Not with this new book contract hanging over her.

AT the stroke of nine-thirty, here came Rosa and the struggle was on. She smiled into the hall mirror and called, "Right on time, as usual." She hung her coat (Donna Karan) in the closet, stashed her handbag (Furli) on the top shelf, changed from her spike heels (Manolo) into sneakers (unidentified), and walked into the kitchen where she found Virginia at the breakfast table, drinking orange juice, fresh from the juicer on the counter, not from one of those waxy cartons no telling how old and soured. Rosa liked that. She would never work for trashy people.

"Slept late, did you?" she said. "I wish I could."

That Virginia had worked until nearly three the night before, trying to meet her deadline, was none of Rosa's business, but

Virginia didn't want Rosa to think she had just been lying abed. "I worked very late on my book."

"How's it going?"

"Sometimes yes and sometimes no." Virginia wouldn't talk about the book with Rosa. Rosa would be full of suggestions as though she were an editor or a writer. "Coffee?" She gestured toward the stove. "Bacon?"

"I've had breakfast. Believe me, I couldn't get here if I didn't have something in my stomach. It's a long trip and standing up all the way. The subway gets worse every day. You're lucky you don't ride it."

Virginia heard judgment ringing in Rosa's tone. "I do ride it," she protested. Her publisher was near Union Square and how could she get there in less than an hour except on the subway? Or to Midtown in less than forty-five minutes? "Of course I ride the subway."

"Not in rush hour you don't," Rosa said, her tone dismissive. "It's different then. A zoo. Animals. They should be locked up in cages. People crawling all over each other like a bucket of worms, jabbering away, pushing and shoving. You're lucky I got here." She launched into the story of her morning, an old man who grabbed her you-know-where, a young man who told her to go you-know-what herself, a little dried up yellow woman shouting at her in her high-pitched Chinese singsong. Rosa blew air through her nose contemptuously. "Stupid people can't even speak English." She drew a deep breath, as though preparing to charge on with the story. "Today was the worst."

Virginia pushed away the orange juice and stood up. With her editor breathing down her back, she didn't have time to listen to the saga of Rosa's morning. "New York can be brutal," Virginia said, hoping that would be the end of it.

"Ha!" Rosa laughed and shook her head. "Not for you, it isn't.

You don't have to mix with those people. You were born lucky, Mrs. B. You got to admit you were born lucky."

Virginia felt miffed by that—as though lucky were somehow a moral failing. She could have told a few stories when she hadn't been lucky—a date rape when she had been a freshman at Bennington, her drawer bulging with rejection slips when she had tried to write for grown-ups, a thousand minor mistakes and mishaps. Still, she knew that if there had been a competition for worst-luck, Rosa would win hands down. "Yes, I guess I was born lucky." With this concession, maybe she could get away. She started toward her workroom.

"I sure wasn't." Rosa went to the sink and poured detergent into the iron frying pan. "I've had to work since I was eleven when my mother died."

There was no way Virginia could just walk out with that statement hanging in the air. "That must have been very hard," she said.

"It was. But I managed." As she scoured the pan, Rosa said that to stay alive it was either sell herself to the tourists as a lot of girls, and some boys, too, did or find something else to sell. "Every day I'd go up to where Manila's garbage was dumped and pick out anything I could sell. See a little glint at the top of a pile of fresh garbage, and I'd go for it, fish heads and dirty diapers up to my knees. I was hoping aluminum, but more likely turn out to be just a tin can full of worms and beetles. But I'd wash it out and sell it and make a few pennies. Once there was a rat in a big tomato juice can. He tried to bite me, but I grabbed his tail and threw him to the other side of the mound. And then I sold the can."

A shiver rose up Virginia's neck. Rosa had told many stories of her life in Manila, but never anything this horrible. A little girl alone in a wicked world, wading knee-high in slime and filth, flinging away a vicious rat. Yet she had managed somehow not to be destroyed by it. There was, Virginia thought with a sudden rush of emotion, something heroic about Rosa, brave, even noble. She put her hand on Rosa's shoulder. "That's so terrible," she said. "I don't believe I would have survived."

"I *know* you wouldn't have," Rosa said. "You'd have died, easy life you've had."

And the moment was over. It was always that way with Rosa. You say something nice, pay her a compliment, and she turns it against you. The more sympathy you showed, the more arrogant she grew. Virginia removed her hand. "Well," she said with a smile that felt like paste around her lips, "I can't imagine how you managed." She began to sidle toward the door.

"I'll tell you how," Rosa quickly said. "I saved all my pennies, nickels, didn't buy that cheap stuff the other girls bought. By the time I was twenty-three I had enough to come to America." She frowned and shook her head. "But that very first year in New York was terrible—I never told you about Antonio, did I? "

"No, but can you tell me later?" Virginia said. "I need to use the bathroom." And with an apologetic grimace that said This is urgent, she disappeared through the doorway.

ROSA was angry. The woman couldn't wait one minute to hear the end of the story? Rude, that's what she was, for all her fine airs. Rosa rinsed out the frying pan and carefully dried it. No one could blame her if it rusted.

As she put the pan in its place in the cabinet, she was thinking about Antonio. Maybe it was a good thing she hadn't told Mrs. B about him. It would have given the wrong impression, that Rosa was a fool. And it didn't matter any more what had happened with Antonio, because she had sure learned her lesson. Now there wasn't a man in Manila or New York or the whole United States—whole world—she'd trust. Finished with that, thank God.

Several strips of bacon were draining on paper towels on the

counter, and a slice of toast had sprung up in the toaster. If Mrs. B
had ever gone hungry, she wouldn't be wasting good food like that.
Rosa decided she might as well eat it, since Mrs. B had offered.
She folded the toast around the bacon. When she took a bite, the
bacon broke into pieces. Crisp, just the way she liked it. She hadn't
had bacon in a while. One-ninety-five for half a pound? Did those
crooked Puerto Ricans think she was made of money? Bad, ugly
people.

But then she thought of Frankie. Black eyes and gold skin and
the whitest teeth she had ever seen. Two months ago he had offered
to carry one of her grocery sacks. At first she had said No, thinking
he would steal it. But when she saw that angel smile, she couldn't
resist. Even though he wasn't more than ten, he had carried the bag
all the way to the fourth floor and set it down at her door. When
she had asked him his name, he had said Francesco but to call him
Frankie. She had offered him two quarters, but he had shaken his
head and said "I'm out of here," and had run down the steps. He
had carried her groceries again the next week, but that time he
had come into her apartment, and she had opened the package
of doughnuts and given him one and a Pepsi. Every Saturday after
that he seemed to be waiting for her when she bought her groceries. He carried them home and came in and had a doughnut and
a Pepsi. He talked about school and what games he liked to play
and once he had told her the whole story of a pirate movie he had
seen. He was so smart. And when he was ready to leave, she took a
damp cloth and wiped the doughnut's powdered sugar off his chin.
Maybe this week she would splurge and buy a chocolate cake and
then she would wipe the chocolate off his chin.

As she gathered up the wet towels in the bathroom and stuffed
them into the hamper, she began to think about the son she might
have had if Antonio hadn't taken her to that wicked doctor. He
would be grown now, and have a wonderful job and be living in an

apartment as beautiful as the Bs'. He would never have been like the hoodlums outside the bodega, grabbing old ladies' purses and selling drugs and having babies that welfare had to look after.

Once she had stopped and told the hoodlums they should be working, and one of them had unzipped and taken out his thing and asked if she had a job for him. They'd all laughed, and she had hurried away, her face burning. Later she had thought what she should have said: That teeny tiny little thing wouldn't do a speck of work for me. She laughed as she imagined the look on his face. That would have shut him up for life.

What chance did Frankie have, growing up around those hoodlums? She had told Mrs. B about him, and Mrs. B had been very interested and had said he sounded like a wonderful boy. Rosa thought that if she worked it right, brought Frankie over to meet them, the Bs would love him as she did and then they would do something for him. They were good people and maybe they would send him to a private school so he could escape the rotten neighborhood. And then they'd send him to college at MIT, where their son had gone, and he would learn all about computers. No, not MIT—it was too far away in Massachusetts and she'd never see him. Columbia, maybe, where Mr. B had gone. And when Frankie graduated in his black cloak and that flat black hat they wear, she and the Bs would be there and he would come to where she sat and kiss her and thank her. And she would say, Dear boy, you're quite welcome but you must also thank the Bs. The Bs were good people and they deserved some of the credit.

She rolled the clothes hamper into the laundry room and dumped it over to separate out the whites. Mr. B wore white jockey briefs and once she had seen a smear of shit on one pair. She laughed, remembering that. With all his fancy manners and all his money he couldn't even keep himself clean. It was disgusting, handling other people's stinking clothes. Not that she would ever mind washing Frankie's. He could bring them to her every weekend. There wouldn't be any shit on them.

VIRGINIA slipped down the hall to her study, to work on her new book, *Two's Company*. She spent ten or so minutes carefully examining the drawings she had already done, adding a little color here, smudging a line there, getting in the mood. This was the one that would do it, win her a Newbery or a Caldecott. Hey, why not a Nobel? She laughed, remembering that she had once thought it might be a Nobel. When she had first begun to write and had just read *Faustus* she had asked herself whether she would choose love or genius if Mephistopheles offered her the choice. What a fool she had been. Cursed with a small talent, she had settled for love, and that had worked well enough, better than most—if she didn't think about that stupid secretary. The male climacteric: a new job, a new locale, or a new wife. That's when they had bought this place. So far so good. And she was happy working, though her creations were not Anna and Vronsky but Mabel Mouse and Dennis Dog. Well, she sure wouldn't win any Newbery if she didn't write it. She slid the top off the box of crayons.

Mabel and Dennis are great pals and often tease Carmel Cat by dancing the tango around the kitchen, dipping and twirling and laughing. Now that had been great fun to draw. Big Dennis swooping down and placing little Mabel on his paw so she could dance as his partner, while off in the corner yellow-eyed Carmel seethes so that her whiskers seem to be vibrating. One day when Dennis is asleep, Carmel goes after little Mabel. That's where Virginia had stopped at three o'clock the night before. Now she prepared to draw the next scene, when Mabel comes awake as Carmel's claws are descending toward her.

Virginia selected a gray crayon with a pinkish tinge that added a little life to the gray. She bent down to her drawing board and began to sketch in Mabel's head. The door opened and there was Rosa.

"You don't mind if I just take a minute, do you?" Rosa said. She was carrying a bucket of water and cloths. Without waiting for an answer, she set the bucket down and began to flick a cloth over the chair rungs and then leaned over Virginia's shoulder to dust the top of the drawing board. "What's that thing?" she asked, pointing the dust cloth at the illustration.

"A mouse." Virginia set the crayon back in the tray and rested her hands in her lap.

"That's supposed to be a mouse?"

Virginia felt the heat rise into her face. "I'm not trying to make it photographic." She sounded more defensive than she intended, and so she added, "Stylized, to give the mouse some individuality, personality."

"Looks kind of pink." Rosa peered closer and laughed. "I never heard of a pink mouse."

"There's always a first time for everything." Virginia blew off the flecks of dust that had fallen from Rosa's cloth onto the drawing. "And it isn't pink." The look she had imagined on Mabel's face was fast receding. A few seconds more of Rosa and the vision would be gone.

"You know, I could write a really interesting book," Rosa said, running her cloth over the top of the drawing board. "Life I've led."

"I'm sure you could." Now go, Virginia thought. Just get out of here.

"My book would be for grown-ups, not little kids," Rosa said. "Nothing fancy, nothing what did you call it? Stylized? No. Just the truth, like little girls selling themselves or living off the garbage. People would be really interested in that."

Virginia leaned closer to the drawing. Was the head all wrong, the nose too pointed, the ears grotesquely large, like stupid Mickey

Mouse? Maybe she would have to start all over again, reconceive the whole stupid book. Weeks wasted. "I wish you wouldn't come busting in when I'm working," she said.

"What?" Rosa took a step back.

"This isn't diddling," Virginia's voice rose, "though you seem to think so. This is my work and I need quiet and privacy. And mice are not all the exact same color. So please don't come in here annoying me with your opinions."

Rosa drew herself up and lifted her chin. "I apologize if I'm bothering you. I'm just trying to do *my* work. I didn't know I wasn't allowed to speak. Yes, I can come back. It doesn't matter if I'm late getting home. That isn't as important as a pink mouse." And she was out the door.

That's it, Virginia thought. The situation was intolerable. It was bad enough to have her breakfast ruined, but now her work. Though Rosa had often come in while Virginia was working she had never commented on a drawing before, never laughed at one, never presumed to judge. So arrogant, so full of herself. Rosa had to go. No matter the book deadline, no matter an inch of dust on every surface, no matter the dirty laundry piling up. She'd give Rosa a month's pay, wish her well, say goodbye. Today. Now. Virginia took the checkbook out of the drawer and wrote out Rosa's wages. Damned if she would put up another moment with that obnoxious woman.

Rosa was finished. She would never allow that woman to yell at her again. She'd quit, walk out. And she wouldn't lower herself to demand to be paid for the half-day though she was owed it. Let the bitch choke on the money. That woman had never done a day's work in her whole life. Playing with crayons like a little baby, drawing stupid pictures that didn't look anything like what they were supposed to. A pink mouse? Ha. And then saying, Get out, when Rosa was just trying to do her work, earn the little bit of money she was paid. That woman didn't care that Rosa would be late getting home. Just cared about herself and her stupid books that not even a five-year-old would like. Rosa slammed the bucket down on the kitchen floor with such force that some of the sudsy water splashed out. Let that woman mop it up.

WHEN Virginia finished writing the check, she took a quick look at the drawing. Perhaps Mabel's color was a little off, the gray-pink too upbeat, almost frivolous. A tad of yellow might add the right tone. She picked up a yellow-gray crayon from the box and sketched in over the pink. Not bad. This made Mabel look jittery, as though her fur was gooseflesh. Virginia began to color in the rest of Mabel's body, first with the pink-gray, then little tinges of the yellow-gray. She stepped back to take a look. Rosa had been right: Mabel had been too pink.

My goodness, how awful to be arguing with the help. They had these little misunderstandings occasionally, when Rosa over-stepped. But had she been too quick with her anger? Had she been rude to Rosa? All the woman had done, really, was comment on the drawing. She shouldn't have, but would firing her be the right thing? Lawrence would complain at the dust accumulating, the laundry not done. She had to acknowledge that Rosa was wonder-ful help, so meticulous, proud to make the place shiny and clean, working even as she talked. Rosa was an honest person, a good per-son, making her way all alone in a foreign country. And there was that little boy she found so fascinating and wanted to help. Suppose she couldn't get another job. Even if she did, some of those agen-cies were robbers, their clients little more than indentured servants. Oh, yes, Rosa could be obnoxious, but being obnoxious hardly jus-tified firing her—particularly when she herself was so very pressed by the book deadline.

Rosa went to the hall closet. She would be glad to be free of this stupid job and that spoiled, useless woman pretending that playing with crayons was work. Probably have a heart attack if she tried to scrub a floor and faint if she ever saw shit on a pair of underpants. Rosa told herself she would never work again for anyone who stayed home and made trouble. At all her other jobs the people were off at work and left her check on the hall table. She'd find something else for Tuesdays.

She leaned against the doorjamb and untied her sneakers. "I'm out of here," she said. That's what Frankie said after they had finished with their Pepsis and doughnuts. Maybe she wouldn't buy the chocolate cake until she got another Tuesday job, but she'd still have doughnuts on Saturday. Frankie expected it.

But what about his schooling, what about college? She had intended to bring him to see the Bs very soon, to get things started. She was sure they wouldn't be able to resist him. Mr. B would know which private school was best for Frankie and they would be happy to pay the tuition. After all, both their kids were computer people and didn't need money. And to be honest, Mrs. B was a generous woman. When Rosa stayed a few minutes late to do special jobs, polish the silver or clean out the closets, Mrs. B always gave her an extra twenty dollars. Not really a bad woman.

Rosa tried to remember whether or not she had said she was quitting. Of course she was glad she had let Mrs. B know she was furious and wouldn't allow anyone to speak to her that way. But she was pretty sure she hadn't said anything definite about quitting.

Virginia tore the check into small pieces, dropped the pieces into the wastebasket, and turned again to the drawing. At a good stopping moment, she would invite Rosa to join her in a cup of tea. When she had a book deadline, she didn't get out during the day and actually it was nice to have someone in the house with her.

———

ROSA retied her sneakers and went back to the kitchen. She took a cloth from the tray and mopped up the spilled water. Perhaps before she left today, she'd ask if she could bring Frankie to meet the Bs. She was sure Mrs. B would adore Frankie.

Bridge

NORMAN HAD BEEN an actuary, quite successful, and quite happily married as those things go. He had expected to die before his wife, Betty, and was at something of a loss when that did not happen. The everyday of his life bewildered him, and he slowly lost weight on frozen food, the dust devils grew into mountains under his bed, and the only people he saw were his neighbors mowing their lawns and the postman delivering junk mail. The empty house felt like a vast and frigid cave.

After Norman had moped around for four months or so, his son, who lived in a distant city, persuaded him to move to a retirement community where he would be entertained and cared for and the son would not have to worry about him anymore. Norman had visited Ridgeside Retirement Residence, had found the food more palatable than frozen chicken dinners, and enjoyed being fawned upon by the rather buxom assistant manager. And so he sold his house, bought an apartment at Triple R, and moved in.

This assistant manager was a good-hearted calculating soul. She knew that if she left Norman just lying around for more than a few days, he'd be snagged by the most acquisitive of the Triple R widows. She had a better use for him than that. As they rode the elevator up to the freshly painted apartment, scrubbed clean of all evidence of the deceased who had occupied it and where Norman would live until he needed to go to the infirmary, she stole a glance at him. He was no beauty, rather chinless, and so thin and bony that it looked as though a coat hanger was holding up his jacket. But she had a plan, and beggars can't be choosers. "Do you play bridge?" she asked.

"Oh, sure," Norman replied.

The assistant manager knew from his tone that he really wasn't much of a bridge player but being male didn't want to admit there was anything he didn't know or couldn't do. "Well, then, you'll be very popular here," she said with a sly wink.

After the first two days during which Norman condensed his seven rooms of furniture to fit into a one-bedroom apartment and sent the rest and most of his books and mementoes into storage so that his son could throw them away when the time came, he was once again at a loss for something to do. So he went wandering around the Triple R premises, pretending to examine the poolroom, the pool, the putting green, none of which interested him in the least. He walked out to the edge of the Triple R grounds, thinking he might investigate the slight incline that lay beyond a thicket of vines and thorns. But he realized that the thicket concealed no telling what vicious snakes and rats, and so he turned away and continued his aimless walking around the manicured lawns.

Three elderly widows—Millie, Jean, and Charlotte—were sitting on the stone bench in the rose garden. The sudden death of their bridge fourth, Angela, had left the three feeling restless and querulous. For nearly five years they had had their daily bridge game, something to look forward to in the morning, something to occupy the afternoon, something to rehash over dinner and through the evening. Of course, they had occasionally had their little unpleasantnesses. When someone fails in what should have been a lay-down slam, the partner would have to be a saint not to express at least a tad of resentment. But if given a choice in a secret ballot, they would probably have preferred each other's company to that of anyone else, including their children and even their grand-children.

From time to time one or another roused herself to speak. Millie pointed out the deadheads the gardener had as usual failed to remove. Jean lamented that her children had missed their last visit. Charlotte declared that Triple R's menu had been exactly the same for three months. Their daily bridge game had held their lives together and without it, each felt quite alone on her own little island.

As the assistant manager was taking a break from planning Triple R's next social gathering, she glanced out the window, and there was Norman and there were the three bridge players. She had been worried about the women ever since Angela had been "called away on more important business," as she called it. Now the hour to solve two problems had struck, and she came whirling out of the building, calling, "Norman. Norman, I want you to meet some wonderful people."

Norman turned around and saw the assistant manager standing beside three elderly women. He thought the women looked quite nice, all in flowery pastels, and since in his sixty hours at Triple R, the only words he had spoken were "I'll have the roast beef" the first night and "I'll have the shrimp" the second, he was glad to have his lonely walk interrupted. He quickly joined the little group.

The assistant manager introduced him by his full name and the women by their full names, then pointed at each in turn and said all the first names again, and to be absolutely sure the names had stuck in those over-stocked heads, she then addressed each individually. "Jean, in August we're having our picnic for all the grandchildren. Oh, Charlotte, we're serving cracked crab tonight, and they look lovely. Millie, the gardener has promised to be more vigilant about the deadheads. Norman, I imagine these ladies would love to play bridge with you."

Norman nodded happily. He hadn't played since high school, but he was pretty sure he could pick it up quickly. "Sure, any time."

The three women looked at each other, silently sharing their thoughts. They had all been widows for a great long time and had come to relish their independence, no one to baby and fawn over, no one to fool into thinking he had had his way, no one to please but themselves and their bridge partner. But what if that partner were male? He would probably change the chemistry of their play, he would probably overbid and steal the contract, and he would no doubt preen like a peacock. So which would be worse, their eyes asked, to allow a man into their game or to have no game at all? They thought of the long empty days.

And so an afternoon game was arranged, and the assistant manager skipped happily away.

A FEW minutes before two that afternoon the three women gathered in the card room to await Norman. Jean roamed nervously around the room. Millie looked out the window to check whether the deadheads had been removed. Charlotte immediately sat down at the table and laid out a hand of solitaire.

"He's so funny looking," Jean said. "Remember Andy Gump in that comic strip? The fellow with no chin?"

"Andy Gump? That must have been before my time," said Millie, with a sweet smile. She was the smallest of the three and generally accepted to be the prettiest. Her skin was soft and fair, her cloud of gray hair well constructed, and her voice so delicate that everyone had to strain forward to hear her. Her husband had bragged that he had married the last of the Southern Belles. She had long since given up ever finding his like again.

"It isn't a question of chins," said Charlotte, placing a red jack on a black queen, "but what bidding system he plays." Charlotte was the largest of the three and the youngest by a year or two. Widowed in early middle age and childless, she had fulfilled her lifelong ambition to become a lawyer, specializing in divorce. Her great case was an eighteen-million-dollar settlement for the ex-wife of a Silicon Valley genius who was not genius enough to hide his money from a legal whiz like Charlotte. After that triumph, she had retired and moved into one of the larger suites at Triple R. "I hope he's kept up with the new conventions."

"Oh, but surely he has or he wouldn't say he could play, would he?" Millie turned to Jean. "Is it all right if Charlotte and I are partners?"

Jean stopped fidgeting and gasped. "But you know how shy I am," she said. Her voice was tentative, as though she were not really hopeful of getting her way. Getting her way had been rare in her marriage to Edgar, a very important heart surgeon. A wonderful, capable man, she always said. But sometimes she thought that he should have let her make a few decisions so that she would have been better prepared when he died. "I think one of you should play with what's-his-name. At least the first time."

"His name is Norman." Charlotte slapped a black ten on the red jack, and in a voice that said she was neither silly nor afraid she repeated. "Norman. Norman. I'll be his partner this time."

As Norman entered the bridge room, it shot through his mind that this was like going on a blind date. He had met Betty on a blind date, but that hadn't been three to one. He didn't much like being outnumbered by these strange women, but, still, playing cards would be a lot better than skulking around the premises. He glanced from one to the other. The little one was pretty, the big one handsome in her way, and the middle one pleasant-looking. He felt livelier than he had in months.

Charlotte gestured him to the empty chair opposite her. "Do you play a weak two?" she asked.

Norman looked at her. "Well," he said, "if that was the contract, I'd have to play it, wouldn't I?"

Charlotte frowned. "I meant opening the bidding with a weak two."

Opening with a weak two? Norman had no idea what that meant. "Depends on the circumstances," he said.

"Of course it depends on the circumstances." With a sharp look at him, Charlotte dealt out the cards.

No one bid on the first hand, and the four threw their cards face up on the table. Millie pointed at Norman's cards. "You had a very good bid," she said.

"You and Charlotte could have easily made four hearts," Jean said.

"Yes," said Charlotte in a rather tight voice. "Deal, Millie."

On the next hand, Millie and Jean bid and made seven spades. "If you had led a club, we would have set them," Charlotte said to Norman.

"If the little dog hadn't stopped by the tree, he would have caught the rabbit," Norman said, laughing.

Jean smiled at Norman. "Good one," she said. She had always laughed at Edgar's sallies. Charlotte frowned at Jean, and Millie rolled her eyes.

On the next hand, Millie played three no-trumps and made two extra tricks. "You could have set us, Norman," she said in a very sweet voice, "if you'd played your king when Charlotte led spades."

Norman looked at her. Melanie on the outside, Scarlett O'Hara within. Norman smiled. That would have been a good one to tell Betty.

"Yes, what on earth were you thinking?" asked Charlotte. What an old battle-axe she was. That was a word Betty's mother used to say. Battle-axe, like something from the Middle Ages or a movie. "Don't you play third hand high?"

"I guess I wasn't thinking," he said. When Jean laughed again, Norman looked at her, wondering whether she was quite all there. Giggling like an idiot. Betty had never giggled. She either laughed or she didn't.

And so it went, one hand after another. Once when he passed Charlotte's one bid, she made a slam. Once he bid out of turn. Once he bid a slam and went down six tricks. Once he reneged.

Millie's voice became much softer, so that Norman had to say "What? What?" every time she bid. Jean giggled after each hand, and Charlotte's lips had completely disappeared inside her mouth and her knuckles were white.

What had he let himself in for? Why were they so angry? Why were they all against him? He felt that he was like a Hollywood hero, fighting off the enemy. Barbaric hordes assaulting the ramparts of the Triple R. That would have been a good one to tell Betty. He began to laugh.

The three women shot quick knowing glances at each other. This fool seemed to have no idea how to play the game, yet he was laughing as though anything he did was just dandy. Typical male defensive arrogance. That busybody down in the main office should mind her own business, if she had any. They should have tried three-handed bridge, maybe hearts or rummy or even taken exercise classes. Anything would be better than to participate in this desecration of the beautiful game.

As he dealt out the cards, Norman was glad he had on a sweater so the women wouldn't see the giant moons expanding under his arms. Betty would never let him wear a blue shirt if he were going to be in a tight situation. Had he really been so lonesome he was willing to be humiliated by these viragos, that simpering fool, that jail warden, that poisonous butterfly? The rats and snakes in the underbrush would be preferable. Better he should join the old men falling asleep on the putting green or play pool or billiards or whatever the hell it was. Triple R had been a terrible mistake. He'd go ask that big woman at the desk if he could get his money back.

He snuck a look at his wristwatch. Jesus. He hadn't been there even an hour, and they expected him to play for at least two hours. He couldn't decently quit. Unless he was sick. Maybe he could pretend he was coming down with a cold. Just the ticket to get him out of this mess. Old folks hated anybody with a cold.

Norman buried his head in his sweater sleeve and emitted a tiny "Snish-snish." And throwing his voice through his nose, he said, "I think I may be coming down with something." Then he let out an enormous "Whoof" and then an even louder "WHAA."

"*Gesundheit*," Jean said, patting his arm.

Gesundheit. Gesundheit was what Betty always said when he sneezed. *Gesundheit*, sweetie. Playful yes, but showing sympathy. She was always aware of him wherever he was and whatever he did, even something as trivial as a sneeze. She had been a loving, kind woman, so unlike these bitches. He should have died first. A woman could manage alone better than a man could. Everybody knew that. But she was gone and he would never see her again. For the years he might still have to live, he would be at the mercy of people like these awful women. His life would be pointless and empty.

The tears welled up in his eyes and then came pouring down his cheeks. "I want my Betty." His shout rang the metal light above the table so that it vibrated from side to side. He crumpled down in his chair and buried his face against his arms, and let loose loud, gasping sobs.

The women were perplexed. Why was he so upset? Was it the bridge and his being so rotten at it? Had they done something to bring this on? Had they been hard on him? Was it their fault? As they exchanged glances, they began to feel quiverings of remorse. They had not meant to drive him to this, only to let him know what a rotten bridge player he was. Perhaps they should have known from the beginning that he couldn't play, that he was pretending so he could have company. He was just lonely. That was the problem. This poor man had reached out to them in his desperate loneliness, and they had failed him.

Millie handed Norman the lace handkerchief she always carried tucked up her sleeve. Charlotte leaned across the table and laid her palm on his head as though in benediction. Jean massaged his hand as she had Edgar's that last night.

Norman looked up at them, his brimming eyes like deep blue lakes. "You're so sweet," he said, "like Betty," and then the lakes were overflowing once more and his head was again buried against his arms. No matter how hard he tried he could not stifle his sobs.

The women were not surprised by this fresh onslaught of tears. Men were just not as strong as women. Oh, Fritz had made a ton of money, Edgar had been the chief of cardiac surgery, and Tom had been the one who always wanted to make love, but they were all basically frail and would never have been able to cope alone. That's why God had decreed that women live longer. Women were more resilient, quicker to right themselves, better able to discover a new life, as they had discovered each other and the blessed bridge.

They began to pat him and murmur soothingly. He had done his best, after all. It was not his fault that he couldn't play. He wasn't dumb. Surely he could learn. They would teach him, and the bridge would save him from despair. And they would have their game.

Untangled

IT WAS LATE afternoon, and a woman stood on a fourth floor balcony of Ridgeside Retirement Residence. She was very thin and rather stooped. Her face was carefully made up with a pale lipstick and a brush of pale rouge, and her white hair was pulled severely back into a coil on the back of her neck. She was leaning over the railing and looking down into the palm-lined driveway. With an impatient shrug she glanced at the tiny silver watch on her wrist.

A yellow taxi drew to a halt in the driveway, and a man slowly emerged from the passenger side, hoisting himself on a silver-headed cane. He was wearing a gray summer suit and a bright red-and-blue necktie with a matching handkerchief stuck into the coat's breast pocket. "Mrs. Upjohn is expecting me," he said to the doorman. Just before he entered the building, he smoothed down his thin, fading pinkish hair, patted his necktie, and tilted up his chin, like an actor preparing an entrance to a stage.

When the man disappeared under the porte-cochere, the woman turned from the railing and went inside. She walked to the sofa and pulled an errant feather from the fabric, shook out the pillows, and plucked at the vase of flowers on the coffee table. From a side table, she picked up a photograph of a man and used the cuff of her silk blouse to dust the glass and the silver frame. When the doorbell chimed, she took a deep breath and started down the hall. As she passed the large gold-leaf mirror in the hallway, she glanced at herself and quickly twisted a few stray strands of hair back into the coil and then lifted her lips in a smile.

"My goodness," the man said when the woman opened the door, "it's so wonderful to see you." He moved toward her, his hands outstretched as though to embrace her.

The woman stepped back and held out her hand. "And to see you," she said.

"A handshake?" the man cried, with an aggrieved though amused look. "Is that how you greet old friends?"

"Those I haven't seen in fifty years, yes," she said.

He laughed and shook his head. "I see you haven't changed one whit in that fifty years."

"Nor have you. Still the flatterer."

As they shook hands they exchanged smiles, his hesitant but friendly, hers stiff and a little wary. "Please come in," the woman said.

The man walked in front of her down the hall. He stopped in the middle of the living room as though to take a reckoning. His gaze traveled the room from object to object, from the sea-green chairs to the green-and-red rug to the large painting of bright diagonal lines. "Very nice," he said. "Your taste has improved."

"What?" The woman's voice was sharp.

"Ah, yes, your taste was egregious—don't try to deny it." He turned to face her, laughed, and shook his finger in admonition. "I remember how you loved those paintings of sad-eyed little girls. You had a reproduction in your dormitory room."

The woman frowned, but then she smiled faintly and said, "Is one never free of the past?"

"Most certainly not."

The woman shrugged. "Well, if my taste has improved, give credit to Andrew." She gestured toward the photograph on the side table. "He educated me."

The man drew back his head and raised his eyebrows. "Does all the credit go to him? Did I have no part in it? Do I get no credit after how hard I worked?"

She shook her hands in the air, waving him off. "Oh, you, too, of course. I was a barbarian, no denying it. You made me throw away that awful picture and gave me a little seascape, all blues and whites and pale yellows."

He glanced around the room. "Do you still have it?"

"I'm afraid not. In all the moves one makes in a lifetime, things do vanish."

"That little seascape cost me two weeks of my GI bill money."

"It was a very nice little picture." She gestured toward a chair. "Please sit down."

With the support of his cane the man eased himself down to the chair. "I'm glad to see you've done so well for yourself."

"Comfortable," she said.

He smiled. "People who say they're comfortable are usually quite rich."

She sat down on the sofa across the coffee table from him. "Then how about almost comfortable."

As he began to laugh, his breath caught, and then he was choking. He pulled the handkerchief from his breast pocket and pressed it against his lips while he coughed.

She leaned forward. "Can I do something?"

He shook his hand and soon the coughing subsided, and he returned the handkerchief to his pocket. "Just another of age's torments, too many cigarettes, too many martinis. Though you seem to have escaped all that." He cocked his head and peered at her. "You know, if I had seen you on a street in New York or Timbuktu, I would have known you. Something essential and enduring in your face. Great bones, I always said." He smiled but when she didn't respond, he said, "But please don't say you would have recognized me, since I'm a dear friend of my mirror, and mark the ravages on a daily basis."

"Then I won't say it. Tell me about yourself and the past fifty years."

"The vital statistics or what matters?"

"Start with the vital statistics."

The Sorbonne had lasted only a year, he said, but then twelve years in Paris with his first wife—well, he had written her about all that—then sixteen in New York with his second wife, and now in New Mexico with his third. Son Mathieu in Prague, son Carter in Hong Kong, both working for investment firms, making buckets of money they don't have the leisure or imagination to enjoy. Not much time for the old man, he said, with a look of amused regret.

When he had finished his brief recitation, she asked, "Whatever happened to the great definitive study of Henry James in Paris?"

He brushed that off with a flick of his fingers. "That was a fantasy. I finally realized I wanted to *be* James, cavorting with the rich and famous, not just write about him."

"Once when I was in Paris, oh, many years ago, I saw you across the Champs-Élysées."

"What? And you didn't speak to me?"

"The traffic," she said, with a flip of her hand. "You were wearing a rakish cap and carrying a cane." She gestured at the cane lying across his lap.

He lifted the cane aloft. "That one was decoration, this one necessity. Two years ago I was thrown from a skittish young gelding. It almost made a gelding of me."

"What on earth were you doing on a horse at your age?"

He shrugged. "Pretending I wasn't my age, of course. The problem is, as I can't remember who said, you get old but you never get older."

"Back to the vital statistics. Doctor? Lawyer? Merchant chief?"

He laughed. "Not even tinker, tailor, soldier, or sailor. Michele had a boutique in Paris—didn't I write you that? And I was the attraction for all the rich American widows passing through. Actually my second, Dolly, was one of them. And so there was New York and lots of fun and after that Ruth hauled me off to New Mexico. Now your turn, please. I want to know everything."

She told him about law school at Berkeley and meeting Andrew, the law firm the two of them had founded in Palo Alto, raising two daughters, widowhood, five adorable grandchildren seen fairly frequently since they lived minutes away, wonderful kids but rather dreading their teen years.

"My life must seem terribly dull and conventional," she said. "Yours was much more exciting."

He shrugged. "I suppose, but once you hit old age, the party's over and everyone's gone home and you have nothing left but confetti on the floor."

"No compensations?"

He laughed. "Of course. Though Ruth hauled me off to New Mexico more or less against my will, I love it. Great skies and beautiful mountains. No pressure to be something one isn't—not that I ever knew the difference." He paused but when she made no response, he went on. "And people when you want them and not when you don't. And of course the horses. They did add great joy to the last years before they turned on me." He leaned forward. "And you, has your 'conventional' life been good?"

"Wonderful." Again she gestured toward the photograph on the end table. "Andrew and I were very happy. We had a great marriage."

"Ah," he said, smiling. "Don't I get some credit for that?"

"What do you mean?"

"Who was it who said if a second marriage is a success, then the first cannot be thought a total failure? Fitzgerald?"

"You and I were not married," she said in a low voice.

"Close to it. Just not the entanglement."

She looked at him but did not speak. After a silence, he said, "I didn't mean for it to come out quite like that. Of course there was entanglement, much more than." He frowned and shook his head. "How many times have I thought of that awful trip to Tijuana, and that filthy man. You were so brave."

She stood up. "My goodness, where have my manners gone. What will you drink?"

"What?" he said, his voice startled. "I was saying that you were…"

"I think I have all the usual," she said, "Sherry? Wine? Martini?"

He leaned back in his chair, a puzzled look on his face. "Well, okay, but water, please, plain or fizzy." When she questioned that with a lifted eyebrow, he shrugged and said. "I was so far gone that even the old doctor in my little New Mexico town told me I had to quit." He shook his head, his expression playfully mournful. "So I spend my last years cold sober. Rather harsh punishment for petty sins, don't you think?"

"It does sound quite petty," she said as she disappeared into the kitchen.

He frowned for a moment, then shrugged. The light from the lamp was shining on the photograph on the end table. He picked it up and studied it for a long moment. When he shifted the frame his own reflection appeared on the glass. He combed his hair with his fingers and reset his necktie and lifted his lips in a smile and replaced the photograph.

In the kitchen, the woman put ice cubes in two glasses and

poured in bottled water. After a pause she emptied one of the glasses into the sink. Then she pulled down a bottle of scotch from a high shelf. As she poured the scotch into the glass, a smile played around her lips. She put both glasses on a tray and added bowls of cashews and olives and carried the tray into the living room.

"The sun is over the yardarm, as we used to say," she said, setting the glass of water and a tiny cloth napkin on the coffee table in front of him. "Are you quite sure you don't want to join me?"

"Want, yes," he said. "But quite sure."

She lifted her glass in a toast. "Well, then, to a long life."

"To a long life." After he had toasted her, he placed the glass on the little napkin. "It's already been a long life, for both of us."

"Too long?"

"Oh, no—never too long, never long enough. I'm far from ready to die."

"The distinguished thing, didn't Henry James call it?"

"Your wonderful memory is still intact," he said with a nod. "Remember how we used to lie in bed and talk about death? You were so determined to face everything head on. Whereas I thought dying was like sex: if you didn't think about it it would go away."

"Andrew always said if there's no solution, there's no problem, so why think about it at all."

"Exactly. So I never do." He paused. "Except those little flickerings of panic in the middle of the night."

They laughed at that, and then she leaned toward him. "Now tell me why you called me."

He shrugged. "I was in San Francisco, and I wanted to see you."

"You haven't been in San Francisco in fifty years?"

He looked away for a moment. "Well, yes, of course I have. And I've kept track of your whereabouts by the changes in the telephone book." He shook his head. "But I kept not calling you."

"So why now?"

He drew a silver box from his coat pocket and took out a tiny yellow pill. "I think my ticker needs a little reinforcement before we venture onto that terrain." He put the pill on his tongue and swallowed it down with water. "How about you, how's your health?"

"Nothing serious. An ache and a pain here and there. I take enough vitamins and supplements every morning so that I hardly need breakfast before I go down to the gym for my thirty minutes of torture."

He laughed. "You actually do all those gyrations and gruntings? Just like you. Such discipline. It used to shame me."

"Now that we've concluded our medical reports," she said, "let me ask again: why now?"

He sighed and glanced around the room before answering. "I know it's rather a mawkish thing to say, but you're my major piece of unfinished business and with a bad heart, I thought I should. We never really came to closure."

"Oh, but I did," she quickly said. "Long ago. Once I met Andrew, none of all that mattered, so you needn't have worried."

"It's always plagued me," he said, closing his eyes and shaking his head as though in pain. "I've always felt such shame."

After a pause, she said, "Oh, well, if it's absolution you want, why don't we stipulate that you have it."

"That makes it sound awfully trivial."

"Aren't all such things trivial after so much time has passed?"

He looked at her steadily for a long moment. "What I can stipulate is that I was a terrible coward. I simply could not face you. When I left, believe me, I meant to come back. Everything just happened so fast." He shook his head, and pressed his lips tight.

"Oh, I'm so glad you didn't," she said, with a relieved sigh.

He stared at her. "Glad?"

"If you had come back, who knows, I might not have met

Andrew." She waved her hand in the air. "But we don't need to rehash the distant past."

He threw himself back in his chair. "So I've been carrying this burden all these years and that's all it meant to you?"

"I'm sorry if it really continued to bother you," she said, shaking her hand in the air as though batting away a mosquito. "But if you came here to be somehow exonerated, surely you're happy now."

"Yes, of course." He frowned and after a moment said, "But to be honest I'm sad that you forgot me so easily while I've constantly thought of you."

"Constantly?"

He laughed. "Whenever always with pain while you forgot me."

"I didn't *forget* you," she said in an impatient voice. "After all that happened, how could I? I'm not yet in my dotage. Of course I was hurt when I got that little note from was it Gstaad? the ski resort? But I was young and those things don't last."

"Well, it has lasted with me all these years," he said, "and finally I found the courage, however late, to come to apologize for my bad behavior."

"Is that what it was? Bad behavior? Like a boy who sasses his teacher?"

"It was much more serious than that, of course, or I wouldn't be here," he said, frowning. "And frankly I expected that it would have meant more to you."

"You expected me to be still suffering?" Her face tightened, and she leaned toward him. "Was that why you came? To get a booster shot for your flagging ego?"

"What?" he said, raring back. "That's outrageous."

"Why else really would you have come?"

"You keep challenging me. I don't remember that trait in you."

"Experience keeps a dear school, but fools will learn from no other," she said with a dry laugh.

"You may doubt if you will, but the honest truth is that I have never stopped suffering for what I did."

"And so you want sympathy because you hurt me?" She cocked her head and stared at him. "Now that is a great definition of chutzpah."

"Well, I was never lacking in *that*." He leaned back and sighed. "Perhaps guilt has a longer shelf life than hurt."

"Could that be because there's more pleasure in it?" She smiled. "A few drops of guilt might be like the bitters in a Manhattan, adding just a touch of zest."

"That is so unfair." He closed his eyes and shook his head.

"You came seeking fairness? Do I owe you fairness?"

His eyes shot wider. "I came seeking penance," he said in a loud voice, straightening his shoulders so that his chin rose.

"Penance?" she repeated. "Penance shouldn't be easy, should it?"

"Easy?" He puffed out a laugh and rolled his eyes. "I feel as though I've been flayed alive."

"In that case, we're getting closer to even." She abruptly stood up. "I'm afraid I'm being derelict in my hostess-y duties. Would you like an olive? A cashew?"

"What I'd desperately like is a scotch and soda," he said, "but fortunately alcohol is like sex and death. Or have I already said that?" He laughed ruefully. "In any case, I must go. My driver will be waiting." He put one hand on the arm of the chair and one on the head of his cane and thrust himself upright.

"Well, if you must." She made a reluctant face, and then smiled. "You were kind to remember an old friend."

"And you to let me visit."

She led the way to the apartment's front door. "Stay off those horses," she said, wagging her finger at him.

He wagged his cane at her. "Take care of those grandchildren."

A Woman and His Dog

ON THE WAY to the hospital that last night, Martin had said, "Take care of Ozzie," and Lydia had promised she would. A few days later somebody—perhaps their granddaughter who had flown in for the funeral—had taken Ozzie to the boarding kennel. But in her grief, Lydia had not thought of the dog until five weeks later one of the veterinarians called to ask how long he would be boarding there. Lydia was ashamed of forgetting her pledge to Martin and sorry to remember it.

Ozzie was a little castrated gray mongrel with black spots and a black muzzle. He had appeared on their front steps late one evening, half-starved and filthy. A tag on his collar had said "Ozzie." Martin had fed him a bowl of milk and some leftover roast lamb and spread an old beach towel on the kitchen floor. Next day Lydia had tacked notices about the dog on nearby telephone poles and the bulletin board at the local grocery store, but no one claimed him. "Some kid just deserted him once the college was out," Martin said. "I guess he's ours."

"Yours," Lydia said. Though they had had dogs when their children were young, she had never liked them—they smelled and shed and barked and ate unmentionable things. But she did not veto Ozzie, for after the first few days Martin had seemed to come out of his depression. In the year and a half since retiring from his engineering firm, he had grown lethargic and morose, slumped in front of the TV, seldom leaving the house, hardly speaking at mealtime, not very fastidious with his shirts and underwear. Ozzie turned out to be better medicine than anything the doctor had prescribed.

Martin bought a new collar and leash and began to take Ozzie for a long walk every morning. He combed the burrs from Ozzie's coat, fed him morsels from the table, and in the evenings tussled with him over an old shoe. After a week or so, Martin bought a dog bed and set it down in their bedroom so Ozzie wouldn't be lonesome at night. Though Lydia had protested, of course she gave in. Martin had become his cheerful, engaged self again, teasing her about what he called her phylogenic prejudices and grooming Ozzie daily. And so it had gone for the two years she had feared she might not have Martin.

WHEN she brought Ozzie home from the kennel, he leaped out of the car and rushed up the back steps, wagging his rump, grinning and slathering, as though he had been anticipating this moment for the whole five weeks. Lydia opened the door, and Ozzie scurried past her to the bedroom, the living room, the kitchen, finally landing at the front door with his chin on his paws.

"No sense waiting," Lydia said. "Martin won't ever come home again." The words seemed to explode in her skull, and she slumped to the floor, the tears coursing down her face. Ozzie came up to her wagging his tail, and she shoved him away.

That evening she brought the dog bed from the garage and put it on the kitchen floor. She let Ozzie out into the backyard for a few minutes and then closed him into the kitchen. And then as she had every night since Martin's death, she lay in bed for hours, gazing at the shadows the streetlights cast on the ceiling, spinning, spinning. Was there anything she could have done? Had he suffered terribly? Why hadn't she gone first? Why was she alive without him?

At early light she woke to an odd noise, an intermittent harsh sound, like a file over metal. She followed the sound down the hallway and opened the kitchen door. Ozzie flew past her. When she turned on the light, she saw splinters of paint along the bottom of the door and scattered across the kitchen linoleum. Ozzie had scratched gashes deep into raw wood.

When Ozzie trotted back down the hall and into the kitchen, Lydia said, "Damn you," and leaning against the doorjamb to steady herself, she whacked him on the jaw with the back of her hand and sent him sprawling. Once he had righted himself, he stared at her in bewilderment.

Martin's dog. She had struck Martin's dog. Never since childhood had she struck a living creature, yet she had struck Martin's dog despite her promise to take care of him. Martin would be ashamed of her, and she was ashamed of herself. She picked up the dog bed and carried it to the corner of the bedroom, just where Martin had placed it.

After breakfast, Lydia hooked Ozzie to the leash and picked up the newspaper in its blue plastic wrapper, and they set out for the pocketsize neighborhood park where Martin had usually taken Ozzie for an early morning outing, where they always had the place to themselves. The park was edged with trees and thick shrubbery and had a zigzag of paths that marked off a swing set, parallel bars, and a splintery wooden bench. Martin had proudly trained Ozzie to stay in the park, and so Lydia unhooked the leash, and

Ozzie began his explorations, sniffing and snorting at every leaf and plunging his black muzzle deep in the grass to get a better purchase on the odors.

"Hurry up," she said to him as she sat down on the bench. "I haven't got all day."

But that was exactly wrong, for: she did have all day. She had nothing to look forward to but a long expanse of empty time. The visits of friends and neighbors had slowly ended, and the telephone calls from her children had become weekly. Oh, yes, she could fiddle in the garden or sweep and dust the house or try to read a book, but there was not one thing in the world she wanted to do. In her teens, she had often thought she was marking time until her real life began. Now she was marking time until it ended.

SHE walked Ozzie to the park every morning, sat for a few minutes while he roamed, cleaned up after him with the blue newspaper wrapper, and then went home. For a week or so that was their routine. But when an early autumn storm struck and the rain seemed like solid sheets of glass, she said, "I'm not taking you for a walk in that," and shoved Ozzie into the back yard. A few minutes later, she heard him crying at the door and she let him back in. He stood in the middle of the room, jerking spasmodically, a shower of water flying around the kitchen, landing on the floor, the chair legs, Lydia's shoes.

Lydia knew it was her own fault. When it had rained, Martin had put on his Burberry raincoat and snap-brim hat and he and Ozzie walked to the corner or around the block. When they came back, Martin always let Ozzie shake off the rain on the front porch and then had rubbed him with an old towel. That evening Lydia donned Martin's raincoat and hat and walked Ozzie to the corner and back and then dried him as best she could.

———

THE rains cleared and by Sunday the air was warm and dry. As Lydia and Ozzie walked the two blocks to the park, there was not a sound except that of a far-off train. She unleashed Ozzie and sat down to read the newspaper. Seventeen bodies had been found in a grave in the back yard of a North Dakota recluse. Forty-three people had been killed in a suicide bombing in Pakistan. A front-page photograph showed a small boy in Darfur, his belly button like a tennis ball being squeezed from his swollen belly. What a miserable world.

As she refolded the paper, ready to go home, she saw Ozzie disappearing into a cave of shrubs and pine trees in the corner of the park, and thinking to keep him from some awfulness, she went in after him.

This time he had not found anything edible even by his standards but a man lying curled on his side. The man's face was marked with dirt and shiny streaks of dried saliva and red welts where he had pressed against the gravel. It was Gene Clabaugh, whose house was on the street behind Lydia's. He taught at the high school—physics or chemistry—and once he had been a member of the town council.

When she leaned over to see whether he was hurt, she could smell the whiskey, the alcohol-saturated stale sweat, and the acrid odor of vomit. "Gene," she said, "can I help?"

He said, "Lemelone fucker," and swung his arm so that she had to shy away. She grabbed Ozzie by his collar and dragged him out of the dell.

A few years back, she and Martin had gone to a party given by the Clabaughs. The music had been fast and furious, the laughter loud and boisterous, the liquor strong and plentiful, and Lydia and Martin were at least twenty-five years older than anyone else. Youthful high spirits, they had thought, just as when they were young they had given and gone to rowdy parties and occasionally had a hangover. But not in a million years would she have expected to find someone like Gene Clabaugh, a pillar of the community, a presumably respectable man, lying drunk in the dirt and swearing at her.

Jennifer Clabaugh was no doubt worried sick. Despite how embarrassing it would be, Lydia knew it was her duty to tell Jennifer that Gene was in the park. She hooked Ozzie to his leash and on the way home they detoured past the Clabaughs' house. And there was Jennifer out in the yard, on her knees, planting pots of chrysanthemums. "Aren't they beautiful," she called. "I love the bronze ones best." She smiled as though she hadn't a care in the world, and Lydia nodded and walked on. Live and learn, she said to herself.

LYDIA took Ozzie to the park each morning during the week, but the next Sunday morning she wanted to avoid any possibility of again encountering a drunken Gene Clabaugh, and so she walked down into the town's little shopping center.

Starbucks Coffee was on a sunny corner and on the sidewalk there were tables and chairs under striped umbrellas and young men and women talking and laughing. The uphill walk home would be a little tiring, so Lydia decided to have a cup of coffee and rest a little. She tied Ozzie's leash to the only empty table, and she went into the café.

The menu boards were bewildering. She had never heard of all those coffee grinds, from Asia and Africa, nor had she drunk coffee with hazelnuts or gingerbread or Valencia orange juice. "Plain coffee," she told the boy behind the counter, and not to look like a tightwad, she added, "and a bear claw. "

When Lydia took her coffee and sweet roll outside, a woman was sitting at the table Lydia had thought was hers, stooped over talking to Ozzie, scratching behind his ears. She was plumpish, fortyish, and blondish, and she was wearing a bright blue velveteen sweat suit. As Lydia stood with her hands full, wondering what to do, the woman straightened up. "Hey, were you sitting here? Come on. Plenty of room for all of us." She patted the chair next to hers.

Lydia said, "Thank you," and sat down.

"So you're Ozzie's mother."

Lydia was surprised, "You know Ozzie?"

"Oh sure. All us regulars know Ozzie." The woman launched into a story about Starbucks and the new culture of coffee and how people were creating real neighborhoods, real friendships, meeting on Sundays just like old times when people went to church. "Me and Terry never would have become friends with Martin except him and us coming here for the coffee."

Lydia smiled and nodded. Martin had occasionally mentioned the coffee shop and people he met there and more than once had suggested she join him on his walks. She had said she preferred exercising on her stationary bicycle to chasing after a dog snuffling and snorting through the underbrush or making small talk with strangers.

A very large middle-aged man wearing white shorts and a maroon-and-gold USC sweatshirt came to the table with a tray of coffee cups and rolls.

"This is Ozzie's mother," the woman said.

"Pleased to meet you, Ozzie's mother." The man set the tray on the table. "Cinnamon cappuccino coming right up."

"I didn't want cinnamon," the woman said.

The man frowned. "You said cinnamon."

"I said caramel." The woman rolled her eyes. "I had cinnamon last time. You don't listen."

"Women," the man said, smiling ruefully at Lydia. "Can't live with them, can't live without them."

"He didn't make that up," the woman said in a scoffing voice. "That's as old as the hills."

"Did I say I made it up?"

"But you didn't say you didn't so that was as good as claiming you did."

The man's face reddened. "Will you for once in your life just shut up? I got you the coffee and all you do is bitch."

"Now who got up on the wrong side of the bed?" The woman winked at Lydia and laughed. "Just listen to him. Martin always called us the Battling Baxleys. Said our marriage must have been made of re-enforced concrete to hold together like it has, despite you-know-who being so bad-tempered and grumpy."

Lydia could not imagine saying such a thing about Martin, obviously baiting him, nor had he ever told her to shut up. Well, but not in public. She finished her coffee and pushed back her chair. "I'll be off now."

"You haven't eaten but a bite of that sweet roll," the woman said.

"I'm running late." Lydia dumped the coffee cup and the sweet roll in the trash, untied Ozzie, and nodded goodbye. As she turned up the hill she heard the man say in a low voice, "Cork up her butt," and the woman chortled and then called after Lydia, "See you next week?"

Lydia just waved her hand and hurried on. Surely these crude and vulgar people weren't friends of Martin's. She had been embarrassed to be at the table with them, even in the same café. Quarreling. Sniping at each other. And that woman laughing right in the man's face. Now that she thought about it, she remembered Martin had mentioned the Baxleys and said they always amused him. Was their behavior what that psychologist called "games people play"? A kind of performance for themselves and others? Just theatre?

As she turned the corner out of sight, she shook her head. Well, they did put on a pretty good show, better than anything television dished up.

THE next Sunday morning, Lydia headed west toward the hills. The houses she and Ozzie passed were pretty much like the other houses in the little suburban town, pastel and well kept, with flowers and trees in the fenced yards and shiny late model cars in the driveways.

At one house, a woman in a faded green bathrobe was on the porch, stooped over to pick up the newspaper. When she looked up, she called, "Hey, Fritzi, here's Ozzie," and an enormous dog five times the size of Ozzie came bounding out of the house and down the steps to the gate. The two dogs sniffed each other as best they could, given the fence and the mismatch, and moaned in high-pitched friendly voices.

"Now the pups can have a play date," the woman said, tightening the belt of her robe as she came down the steps. "I'm Edie. Come on in."

"Thanks but we have to be going."

"Oh, maybe just a short visit?" the woman said. She put her hand on the gate closure. "Martin and I used to laugh about how different Fritz and Ozzie were, yet such good friends. Fritz has sure missed Ozzie. Two minutes?"

How could Lydia say she didn't even have two minutes when Martin apparently had stopped to let the dogs play? Reluctantly she nodded. Edie opened the gate, and immediately the dogs raced to the other end of the yard, Fritz bounding and leaping and Ozzie motoring along like a wind-up toy. The lawn, Lydia noticed, had large brown spots where the grass had died, no doubt Fritz's work.

"Fritz is pure German Shepherd." Edie looked after the dogs and smiled. "I've always had big dogs."

"German Shepherds?" Lydia said, thinking that little dogs were trouble enough.

"Different kinds," Edie said. "Diarmuid was a Rough Collie— that's a Scotch breed. He was the smartest dog I ever had but you could fill a mattress with the hair he shed. Same for my Malamute. Sakari—that means sweetheart in Inuit and she sure was. I cried buckets when she died. Torkild was a Great Dane, the best looking but dumb as wallpaper. Fritz—that's short for Friedrich, you know, German? He's the bravest."

As they watched the dogs tumbling in the back yard, Edie told a story of how one night when her husband was away and she was alone, a burglar had broken in and Fritz went after him and tore his pant leg and probably some flesh, and the burglar had run from the house. When she had finished her story, she smiled and said, "I don't guess little Ozzie could ever frighten anybody."

"Probably not," Lydia said. "We have to be getting on now." She whistled as Martin did, and Ozzie came running.

"Well," Edie said, "next time plan to come in for coffee so the pups can cavort."

Lydia hooked Ozzie to the leash, smiled at Edie, and started back toward home.

Cavort. Of course Lydia had seen that word in print, but she didn't think she had ever heard it spoken. Pretentious, that's what it was. Why not just say "play" or "race around"? And those names. A German Shepherd with a German name. The collie with a Scottish name Lydia knew she couldn't possibly pronounce, a Malamute named something like sweetheart and the Great Dane was what? Tork-something. Some Danish name, of course. Just imagine the trouble it took to find those crazy names, checking the breed to see which one fit. Edie probably was an educator, maybe a professor at the college. Anyway, educated. And, really, when you thought about it the names were imaginative and kind of fun.

Lydia glanced at Ozzie cavorting in front of her. She should rename him, something fitting his breed. As they turned the next corner, she said, "Well, Mutt, you may not chase burglars, but at least you aren't eating me out of house and home and defecating like an elephant."

And that made her laugh so hard she had to cover her mouth so no one driving by would think she was a lunatic. Ozzie looked up at her, slathering and grinning as though he caught the joke.

THE next Sunday, Lydia lay in bed wondering where she would walk Ozzie this time. They had gone north and found a drunken Gene Clabaugh, east to the Battling Baxleys, and west to Edie and Friedrich. "Shall we go south this time, Ozzie? No telling what we'll come on." At the sound of his name Ozzie leaped up and ran over to her. He put his paws up on the bed, and Lydia reached over and scratched him behind his ears.

Dust Catchers

IF SHE DIDN'T really wake up, she could perhaps go back into her dream. Ivan had looked so handsome in his officer's uniform— pinks they called them. They were driving along Point Reyes in his little Studebaker Champion. The sky was cloudless, the ocean glistening, the white caps rising and falling. Look, he said, pointing at an immense whale frolicking off shore. And then he was shouting angrily and banging his fist on the steering wheel.

Jean opened her eyes. The sun was already streaming through the western windows. Though she had only meant to rest a moment, she must have been asleep on the sofa for hours. Usually people just went away when she didn't come to the door, but this one kept on shouting and knocking until Jean was afraid the glass pane might crack. Perhaps it was important—the house on fire or a message from Carolee or Andrew. She sat up on the edge of the sofa and waited for the throbbing in her head to subside and her eyes to focus. Then holding on to the chair, the highboy, the wall, she began to walk toward the front door.

As she passed the hallway mirror she caught a glimpse of herself. She was still in her nightgown and her old tattered plaid robe. What a sight, she thought, patting down her tangled hair and scraping her thumbnail over the crusts of spit on her chin. She really should freshen up, but there it was again, someone shouting and knocking.

On the other side of the glass door panel was a very large woman with copper-colored hair and a big moon face. Perhaps one of the Jehovah's Witnesses—they sometimes came by, simple, good-hearted women, cheerfully resigned to rebuff. Ivan had once let in a very tall bony young black woman and a very fat old white woman, and for five minutes they had spoken to him about the state of his soul, and he had pretended to be remorseful and eager to be saved. Finally he had tired of the game and told them he couldn't give his soul to God because he had already sold it to the devil for a dollar and fifty cents. The poor things had scurried away, red-faced but still smiling. Jean had said nothing—it would only have made him angry.

"I admire what you're doing," she said through the glass panel, "but I don't discuss religion with anybody."

"What? Religion? You think I'm trying to convert you or something? That's a good one." As the woman laughed her cheeks ballooned and her little eyes almost disappeared and her tongue bobbed up and down. When her laughter subsided, she leaned close to the glass. "You don't recognize me, do you? Lived in the Tudor down the street?"

She pronounced it two-door, like a car, and it took Jean a moment to realize she meant the house with the crossbeams in the next block. The house was dilapidated for the neighborhood, a rental with a constant stream of families passing through. Jean didn't remember ever knowing anyone who lived there, but then her memory wasn't what it used to be, and she wouldn't be rude to an old neighbor. She slid back the dead bolt.

As the woman stepped over the doorsill, her face grew solemn. "I just heard the awful news about your hubby, and I come right over." She engulfed Jean in her immense flabby arms and swayed wordlessly for a minute. She smelled of talcum powder and stale sweat.

Jean's stomach kicked and bile rose into her mouth. Feeling the way she did, she should never have answered the door. She didn't want to see anyone, not until she got herself together. Her neighbors and the people from her church seemed to understand that and no longer came by.

"I know exactly what you're feeling," the woman went on, "because I lost my Warren last year." With a deep sigh of reluctance, she released Jean. "Cancer of the bowel. I won't describe what I went through. It'd make you sick to your stomach. Innards coming out. That was about the awfullest way he could of chose to go. You remember Warren, don't you? My height but real skinny?"

Jean couldn't recall knowing anyone named Warren, but she murmured "Umm."

"Thought you would. Nobody ever forgot my Warren. Cute as a button. Now come on, let's have us a heart-to-heart, beings as we've been through the same thing." The woman walked past Jean into the living room. "I always liked this room," she said. Her gaze hopped from the Oriental rug to the bric-a-brac cabinet to the mantel and the pictures of Ivan and the children. "There he is," she said, pointing at Ivan's picture. "That hubby of yours was more fun than a barrel of monkeys."

More fun than a barrel of monkeys? Ivan was a somber man, moody, not at all social. Days could go by without his saying more than *Pass the salt* or answering *Yes* or *No* to one of her questions.

Jean had learned not to insist, just to walk away. The minister said that was the best thing to do.

"Do you mean Ivan?" she said.

"That's his name, ain't it?" The woman pointed at the pictures of Jean's children when they were little. "And that's...shoot, I can't rightly remember their names."

"Carolee and Andrew," Jean said.

"Carolee, of course." The woman shook her head. "I guess I'm getting forgetful."

"Me, too." Jean smiled. "I can't remember your name."

"Sylvia?" the woman said. "Sylvia Smith? Down the street? Now do you remember?"

Jean nodded though she didn't at all. Since Ivan's death, and really long before, she was slow in recalling things she had once known perfectly well. If she could take one of the orange pills the new doctor had prescribed, her mind would be clearer. "Would you like a cup of tea?" she asked.

"I don't mind if I do."

"Milk? Lemon?"

"I like everything straight—tea, whisky, and men." The woman began to laugh and her face swelled and reddened and her tongue flicked in and out. "Get it?"

Jean said, "Have a seat. I'll just be a minute." She went into the kitchen and put a kettle of water on the burner and set out cups and saucers and some cookies from a box. Then she took a bottle of medicine from the cabinet above the sink. The new young doctor—Carter? Farmer?—had said she could take one of the pills every four hours, and since she hadn't had one since morning and here it was late afternoon, she shook out two pills. She took the gin from under the sink and poured some into a glass and used it to wash down the pills. Gin helped to dissolve the medicine so it acted more quickly.

When Jean went back into the living room with the tea tray, Sylvia had opened Ivan's bric-a-brac cabinet and was holding the gold thimble up to the light.

"You mustn't touch those things," Jean said.

"Them your souvenirs?" Sylvia asked.

The thimble was one of what Ivan had called "my heirlooms," valuables that his family had managed to sneak out of Russia when the Bolsheviks took over. Ivan never let anyone touch them. He dusted and polished them himself and kept the glass cabinet gleaming.

"Ivan's grandmother brought them from Moscow a hundred years ago. Ivan didn't want anyone to touch them."

"And looks like nobody has in a month of Sundays." Sylvia turned from the cabinet and eased herself down at the tea table. "At least an inch of dust."

The best thing to do, Jean thought, was say nothing at all and just let the conversation die, and the woman would leave. She had often done that after Ivan's death, when people were still coming by to see her. She handed a cup of tea to Sylvia and offered the plate of cookies.

Sylvia took a sip of tea and a bite of cookie. She made a hideous face and spat the glob of cookie onto her saucer. "Tastes like a cow pat. Not that I ever tasted a cow pat." She laughed and slapped her thigh, and her copper colored curls shook, and her bright red tongue shot in and out like a live thing. "And just look, this plate has dried gunk sticking to it."

Jean drew in a quick breath and looked down at the teapot. "I'm sorry," she said. "I guess I'm not a very careful housekeeper since Ivan died."

"You ain't kidding," Sylvia said. "But that's not the point. The point is you ain't taking care of yourself and that worries me. I always liked you and we always had good times together, you and me and your hubby. I'll just say it out blunt so's you'll know where I stand. That's just the way I am. I say it like it is. You mentioned religion? Well, I see now that I've been called to save you." She reared back and smiled as though she had just bestowed a high honor on Jean.

Jean wasn't sure she had understood. The medicine was taking too long to act. "Save me from what?"

"From yourself. You ain't doing so good, that's clear as day," Sylvia said.

"That's because I just lost my husband," Jean said.

"Well, you ain't going to find him this way," Sylvia said with another burst of laughter. "Time to move on, and that's where I come in. I'm the kind of person that likes to help the downtrodden. That's just the way I am." She leaned forward and spread her arms as though about to engulf Jean again. "Warren always said that was my biggest fault, wanting to help people. And it's clear as day you're letting yourself go with all this grieving, just like I did. But now I'm here to help you. I'll do your shopping for you, so you won't be eating cow pats, some cooking so you don't blow away like a dandelion, some cleaning so the place don't smell like a toilet."

Jean pressed back against the sofa pillow. Was this the hallucination the old doctor had warned her about? Booze and drugs don't like each other, he'd said. You'll see things you won't like, ugly things. No more pills until I know you're not drinking. Are you trying to kill yourself? Is that what you're doing? He had been unkind, and so she had found the new doctor. Jean forced herself to smile. "It's nice of you to offer," she said, "but I don't need any help. I'm all right."

"You're all wrong," Sylvia said, with a flip of her fat fingers. "You're lonely and you're zonked out on booze and drugs. Like when you were in the kitchen fixing the tea? Took yourself a pill, didn't you? And a snort, too, I bet. Maybe two snorts."

"I took my medicine because it was time," Jean said.

"Your hubby maybe couldn't smell the gin, but I ain't got this nose for nothing." Sylvia twisted her nose this way and that and let loose with her awful laugh.

Jean peered more closely. There was nothing familiar about this woman, not the loud raspy laughter or the copper curls or the moon face. Not even the name. "I don't think I ever knew anyone named Sylvia Smith in my whole life," Jean said. "You never lived around here, did you? You made it all up, Warren and the Tudor."

"That's a perfect example of what's happening to you, your memory's going." Sylvia pressed her lips together and shook her head as though in sorrow. "You need help and here I am, sent by the Lord to help you."

Jean lifted her chin. "I don't need help, thank you."

"You don't?" Sylvia leaned across the tea tray and plucked the edge of Jean's bathrobe. "Well, just take a look at yourself. Wearing a filthy nightie at five in the afternoon. Stinking like a drunken old bag lady. Bet you haven't took a bath in a week. And how many times you turned that sofa cushion because you peed it? You're going to hell in a hand basket, missy."

Jean began to tremble and her breath came short. "I want you to leave," she whispered, and then in a stronger voice said, "Get out of my house."

Sylvia laughed and said. "See? I've made you better already. Put a little gumption in you."

"If you don't leave, I'm going to call the police." Jean reached across the arm of the sofa toward the telephone.

"Don't get your underdrawers in a tangle." Sylvia said. She hoisted herself up and, like a yacht weighing anchor, glided past Jean to the front door. As she opened the door, she called over her shoulder, "It's my Christian duty to look after you, and I'll be back."

When she heard the door closing, Jean fell against the sofa

pillows. That awful woman, that hideous creature, a liar, pretending to be from the neighborhood, pretending to know Ivan. Ivan was more fun than a barrel of monkeys, she had said. That was a barrel of lies. She didn't know Ivan or she would know not ever to touch the heirlooms.

Jean glanced over at the cabinet and noticed that the door was ajar. When she stood up and walked over to close it, she saw a tiny clean circle surrounded by dust where the gold thimble had been. She looked all through the cabinet but there was no gold thimble. The woman had stolen it. Ivan would have been furious. I can't trust you with anything.

Jean went to the telephone to call the police. As she pressed the 9, she rehearsed what she would say. I want to report a theft. A woman stole Ivan's thimble. How absurd the police would think her, to be calling 911 because of a thimble. They would never understand how much Ivan had valued it and how miserable she now felt. She had no idea where the woman lived, or even her real name, though she was pretty sure it wasn't Sylvia Smith. The police would ask why she had let in a stranger, and why was she still in her nightgown, and why she smelled of gin, and they would call Carolee and Andrew.

Jean's hands were shaking as she put the telephone back in its cradle. She had not wanted to look after the heirlooms, but Carolee and Andrew had refused to take them, scoffing at them, saying they were just dust catchers. Perhaps they were. Perhaps the thimble wasn't really valuable, just a little piece of gold plate. She went to the cabinet and blew on the dust to cover the clean spot.

The encounter and then the trouble with the thimble had been exhausting and had left her weak and trembling. That awful woman had called her a bag lady and said she smelled. Jean put her nose to her armpit. Yes, there was a dank, mossy smell. Of course she would have showered, but how could she with that awful woman bursting in. She went back to the sofa and lay down until she could catch her breath. *I'll just lie quietly for a minute or two and then I'll bathe.*

IT was full dark when the telephone awakened her, and she pulled herself up from the sofa to answer it. It was Andrew. For the three months since Ivan's death, he had called every Thursday. "You're like clockwork," she said. "How are you?" She felt a pang of guilt. He would be so ashamed if he saw her in the filthy nightgown, her hair lank and greasy, her chin itching with dried spit.

As he always did, he reported on the week past and the week ahead, his son's exploits on his high school baseball team, the French movie he and his wife had seen, the new wonder product his company was marketing. "How about you?" he asked. "Taking care of yourself? Seeing people?"

For a moment, she thought she would tell him about that woman and the stolen thimble. No—that would worry him and make him think she was incompetent, letting in a stranger. But he would be pleased to know she had had company.

"Yes, I had company this afternoon, an old friend I hadn't seen in a long time," she said, smiling, hoping the smile sounded in her voice. "Every day I feel better."

"I'm glad," he said. "I'll call next week."

It was easy to fool Andrew. He so wanted to believe everything was fine. Carolee was more suspicious. When she had called last Friday she had said Jean's voice sounded slurred, and Jean had quickly said she had gone to the dentist—"First time since your dad got sick"—and her mouth was full of Novocain. Carolee had said she was very pleased to hear Jean was taking care of herself. They were good children, and though Ivan had left them the house once Jean died, Jean's gift to them was not ever bothering them.

It had been hours since she had had any medicine, and the

new doctor had told her every four. No wonder her head was throbbing and her hands were shaking. She went to the kitchen and took down the medicine bottle and shook out a pill. Zonked on pills and booze, that awful woman had said. Zonked? Well, whatever zonked meant, she was not zonked. She took her medicine because the new doctor had prescribed it. Why would you have a doctor if you didn't do what he said?

After she had swallowed down the pill and the gin, she went over to the refrigerator. The new doctor had put his fingers around her upper arm and said, I want you to put some meat on these bones, and she had promised she would. He wasn't mean and judgmental like the old doctor, and she wanted to please him.

She opened the refrigerator and took out a slice of bread and an egg. The bread was stale but it would be all right after it was toasted. She put the bread in the toaster and broke the egg into a frying pan. I'm doing what you told me to, she said to the new doctor. And he would smile and say, Very good, young lady.

As she scooped the egg onto the toast, the yolk broke and the yellow began to ooze across the plate like living slime, and a smell of sulphur rose up. Jean's stomach clenched, and for a moment she thought she would vomit. She quickly sat down and put her head between her knees and took deep breaths.

Once her stomach had settled, she ate the part of the toast that the broken egg hadn't touched and drank half a glass of orange juice. Though it was only eight-thirty, she decided she would go upstairs, take a shower, wash her hair, and sleep in her own bed—she would not sleep on the sofa ever again. She shook out two pills and poured a tumbler of gin, not for now, no, but she would take them with her just in case she woke up during the night and needed them. No point in having to come all the way back downstairs.

She carried the pills and the gin up to her bedroom and put them on the bedside table. As she started to take off her robe and nightgown so she could shower, she realized she couldn't go to bed with her hair wet—it might ruin the pillow and she might catch cold and anyway she was too tired. In the morning she would shower and wash her hair and put on fresh clothes and she would feel good all day. I am not going to hell in a hand basket.

The television remote control was on the bedside table and she turned it on. Some men were playing cards. They looked very scruffy in T-shirts and loud jackets, just the kind of men Ivan despised. She watched for a few minutes, until one of the men stood up and began to shout, and then she clicked on another channel. An enormous loud woman who looked like Sylvia only brunette and short was shouting at an old man and he was shouting at her. Why did everyone shout so?

Jean clicked again and a fawn-colored gazelle with a white chest and beautiful lyre-shaped horns was running through the brush. Jean relaxed back against the pillows to watch the little gazelle. The scene changed and something huge—a lion—leaped from the bushes and grabbed the gazelle and began to tear at its flesh, and the gazelle began to screech. Jean quickly turned off the television, but already her head was throbbing and her hands were shaking. She had promised the new young doctor she would take the medicine only every four hours, and it wasn't time yet. But if she drank a little of the gin maybe she would be able to forget that awful screeching and fall asleep, and tomorrow she would bathe and wash her hair.

"PASSED out, did you? Still in that nasty nightie and just look, you peed yourself again." Sylvia batted her hand in front of her nose. "Can't leave you alone for a minute."

Jean opened her eyes. She was on the sofa in the living room, and there was Sylvia sprawled in the big chair across the tea table. "How did you get in?" Jean muttered.

"If you're going to leave the door unlocked you're lucky it was me come in and not some axe murderer." Sylvia shook her head and her copper curls seemed almost electrified. "What a nasty kitchen. Whoof. God almighty chunks of egg and bread all over the place. I cleaned it all up. See how useful I can be to you? But next time you upchuck try to make it to the sink."

Jean didn't remember coming downstairs during the night or trying to eat, but she still tasted the vomit. "That was just an accident," she murmured.

"Well I didn't think you did it on purpose." Sylvia barked out a short laugh. "Now get up and go to the little girls' room before you pee that sofa again. And take off that nasty nightie while you're about it and get yourself a bath."

"Go away," Jean said. "Please go away." As she sat up, she remembered the thimble, and she thought that perhaps Sylvia was contrite and was returning it. Be forgiving, the minister had told her long ago, just as the Lord forgives us. And she was forgiving. Carolee said so. Andrew said so. "I'm glad you've brought back the thimble." She put out her hand toward Sylvia and smiled. "I won't say a word about it."

"What are you talking about?"

"The gold thimble you took from the cabinet."

Sylvia seemed to swell up to twice her size. "You accusing me of stealing?" She rolled her immense shoulders forward and jutted out her chin, and she looked at though she might leap across the table.

Jean pressed back against the sofa pillows "Of course I'm not accusing you of stealing. I just thought..."—But what could she have thought?—"...that you borrowed it since you said you were coming back."

"I don't need to borrow no thimble. I got a dozen of my own." Sylvia eyed Jean as though deciding what action to take, and then she relaxed back against the chair and huffed out a little laugh. "You better watch that tongue of yours, else we ain't going to get along so hot."

Jean took a deep breath and sat up straighter. "But I don't want us to get along. I want you to leave or I'll call the police."

"I don't think you want to be making any threats." Sylvia narrowed her eyes and they were like laser beams aimed at Jean. "What if your children found out what a mess you are, all them pills and booze and upchucking and peeing all over the place. I wonder if it ain't my Christian duty to tell them."

Jean felt a fluttering in her head, and she was afraid she would pass out again. "But you don't know my children," she said

"Don't I?" Sylvia said with a little sneer. "Carolee and Andrew? That ain't their telephone in this book?" She held up Jean's little address book. "If I call and tell them what's going on here, it would break their hearts."

"No," Jean said, "no, please don't call them." She pressed her hands to her temples to settle the dizziness. "I know we can work this out."

Sylvia sat back. "All's I want is to be helpful. That's the way I am. I care more about others than I do about myself." She waited until Jean nodded, and then she said, "Okay, here's the way it's going to work. You give me three hundred dollars a week—checks are okay—and I'll come over every afternoon about five, fix us some dinner, tidy up the place, make you take a bath so you don't stink so bad, be company for you." She looked hard at Jean. "When's the last time you saw any of your old pals?"

Jean said. "I just wanted to be alone for a while."

"How long a while? Until you croak? Is that what you want?"

Jean said. "Two or three weeks."

Sylvia got up and walked to the bric-a-brac cabinet. "This where that thimble was you say I stole?"

"I misspoke," Jean said.

Sylvia opened the cabinet and took out Ivan's grandmother's cameo with the gold-filigreed frame. "Nice," she said, turning the cameo in the light. Then she pointed into the cabinet. "What's that?"

"It's a Fabergé egg," Jean said. "Ivan said it was very valuable."

"Anybody clean in here in the last century?" Sylvia took a handkerchief from between her breasts and began to smear the dust over the shelf, lifting first one item then another. "You don't need the aggravation, situation you're in," she said, batting away the dust particles that swam in the air. "They're just something more for you to worry yourself with and keep you from doing what you want."

"Yes, they're a burden," Jean said, "but Ivan made me promise I'd take care of them."

"Ivan's dead, ain't he?"

"Yes," Jean said, "he's dead."

"So you're free to do as you please, ain't you? and I bet it ain't looking after these dust catchers." Sylvia turned from the cabinet. "You ought to get rid of them. Now go get us some money so I can buy us something good to eat. There ain't much left in that kitchen and what there is a stray dog wouldn't eat."

"You're right," Jean said as she left the room.

Sylvia had cleaned up the kitchen. The pill bottle was on the counter and the empty gin bottle in the trash and the floor had been mopped. Sylvia was wonderful. Jean took her checkbook from the drawer under the cabinet and made out a three hundred dollar check to cash because she didn't know Sylvia's real name. Then she reached under the sink where she kept the case of gin. There were only three bottles left, but by the time they were finished maybe she wouldn't need any more.

As Jean went back into the living room, Sylvia turned from the bric-a-brac cabinet and laughed. "I hope you enjoyed it." She held out her hand and took the check. "Look, I don't care about the booze and the pills. I just want you to be happy, and I tell you them dusty old souvenirs ain't doing it and if the booze does, then okay. See? I'm kind of your guardian angel."

"I think you are," Jean said.

Once the front door had closed behind Sylvia, Jean looked into the bric-a-brac cabinet. All Ivan's heirlooms had been rearranged after Sylvia's dusting, but Jean realized the cameo and the Fabergé egg and, yes, the pearl tie pin were gone. Sylvia was doing her work more quickly now. Tomorrow perhaps the three little gold demi-tasse spoons with Ivan's family crest and the black fan with the dia-mond decorations and the next day the letter opener with the ruby-and-amber inlay and the letter bearing the seal of the Archduke.

Jean felt a rush of fear and began to tremble. Ivan would be furious. But then she smiled. As Sylvia had said, Ivan was dead and Jean was free to do what she had wanted to do for so many years. And once the hideous heirlooms were gone, she would send the sofa cushions to be cleaned, scour the gunk off all the dishes, and throw the bric-a-brac cabinet in the city dumpster. Everything should be nice for Carolee and Andrew. A widow she knew had had the inside of her house painted and the windows washed, and when she had accomplished that she died.

Regulars

ELLEN SITS IN one of the greasy vinyl chairs in the visiting alcove outside the hospital ward. A book is open on her lap, but she's too restless to read. To while away the time she looks around at the afternoon visitors. A man in a business suit stalks up and down, shooting his cuff to glance malevolently at his watch. Another man, this one in a cowboy hat and boots, sits hunched over, twisting his fingers as though trying to jerk them loose from the palm. A teen-aged girl in jean shorts hanging precariously from her hipbones sighs impatiently, and with each sigh her belly button winks like a third eye. Usually the visitors are there for a day or two and then vanish. Ellen wonders whether the patient has died or the ailment was trivial—a new baby, a broken leg—hardly worth the fuss, the time lost from work.

When a haggard blond woman and a little girl in crisp overalls come into the alcove, Ellen closes her book and stands up. "I'm just leaving," she says. She heads for the swinging doors to the ward. Sometimes she can go in a few minutes early.

THE Intensive Care nurse sits at a wall of computer screens and machines, reading the vital signs of the three patients. Henry is in the bed nearest the door, his eyes closed, his mouth ajar. Tubes dangle from his nose, his mouth, his arm, from under the sheet. There's a glistening trail of spit from the corner of his mouth down his chin. He would hate that. Ellen pulls a tissue from the packet she carries and carefully wipes his mouth. She kisses him on his lips and rests her head against his. There is no response. She knows he is dying and that there is nothing the nurses, the doctors, the machines can do. Nothing she can do.

AS she enters her condo she picks up a box left between the screen and the front door. Godiva Chocolates. Good, she thinks. No wilting flowers and stagnant water to throw out, no soured chicken salad to shove down the disposal. When Henry first had the stroke, their friends came to the hospital to spend long hours with her. But when they held her hand and sympathized and talked about Henry, it took all her energy to control her emotions and not cry. She doesn't want to cry. Even though she knows it's futile, when she goes into the ICU she wants to be upbeat and hopeful, not red-eyed and depleted. It is much easier when she's surrounded by strangers.

After the first three days, she told her friends she needed to be alone at the hospital, and her friends had understood. So now they leave casseroles and salads and flowers at her door. She sets the Godiva box on the coffee table. She'll write a note of thanks later. For now, she just wants to go to bed and try to sleep.

THE weather turns overnight, and it is drizzling by the next morning. After her first visit to Henry, Ellen goes into the empty alcove. She picks up an old *National Geographic* with the corner torn off—the contribution of some doctor not wanting to expose a home address—and starts to read an article on chimpanzees in the Congo.

Soon a man comes in and drops like a heavy sack of flour into a chair. She recognizes the cowboy hat with its stain of sweat around the crown. He was there yesterday and, yes, the day before that and perhaps the whole twelve days that she has been there. About her age, early sixties. Cheeks and chin in need of a shave, light blue shirt in need of a wash. Large bones, leathery skin, shaggy reddish-brown hair hanging below the ludicrous hat. A coarse, ugly man—cousin of a chimp.

She lowers her eyes and tries to read, but the print slips and slides across the page. Why isn't that oaf lying in there instead of Henry? Why isn't he the one dying? What good is he to the world? Her breath catches and her heart begins to beat into her throat. Stop it, she says to herself, get control of yourself. It does Henry no good for her to thrash about at everything. She puts her hand on her thigh and squeezes.

Slowly her breath settles, and after a minute she says, "We seem to be the regulars." It is her way of apologizing for her anger and scorn.

The man looks up. "Yeah, the regulars," he says, with a wry snuffle.

FOR lunch Ellen buys a ham sandwich and a can of V8 juice and sits at a corner table in the hospital cafeteria. When she sees the man in the cowboy hat at the hot food counter, she ducks her head and turns away. But he has seen her, and after he pays for his lunch, he comes up to her table with his tray.

"Remember me?" he says. "One of the regulars?" He plops into the chair across from her and holds out his hand. "Sid Bowen," he says. "Looks like the both of us are in for the long haul, so we might as well get acquainted."

Ellen says her name and they shake hands. Sid picks up his knife and fork and saws off a piece of the pot roast on his plate. He smears the meat with mashed potatoes and gravy and jams the mess into his mouth so that the gravy bubbles up around his teeth.

She waits a few moments and then pats her lips with the shredded paper napkin, and pushes back her chair. "Well, I better be off."

Sid looks puzzled. "But you ain't finished your sandwich," he says, pointing his fork at her sandwich as though she wouldn't have noticed.

She gathers the paper plate and the V8 can and the paper napkin. "I've had enough." She goes over to the garbage bin at the door and drops in the debris. She glances back. Sid is looking after her, puzzled and annoyed. She shouldn't have spoken to him in the first place.

IT'S time for Ellen's last evening visit, but there has been an emergency in ICU—no doubt someone has died—and she must wait in the empty alcove. After a few minutes, Sid Bowen comes in. When he sees her, his expression turns wary, suspicious. She feels ashamed at having been rude to him and she smiles and says, "The regulars."

He sits down across from her. He says it's funny there ain't nobody else in the alcove but the regulars, and she says that most visitors come in the late afternoon and early evening and then go home. He laughs and says he wishes he could go home instead of staying at that crummy motel up El Camino, the Honolulu Inn. He says sometimes he thinks the trucks are right in the room with him and the bed is made of rocks and it takes twenty minutes to get any hot water. "It's a sight worse than it was even six months ago, when me and Louise came down first time to see the specialists at the hospital."

When Ellen says, "So you're not from around here," Sid answers that he has a cattle ranch over near Bodie that his son is taking care of while he's down here. His daughter lives up in Coeur d'Alene, he says, coming down in a day or two to see her mom. "What about you?" he asks.

The exchange of inconsequential personal information, she thinks, that passes for conversation. Well, but what else could they talk about? Politics? Religion? He is probably an evangelical gun owner. They'd be shouting at each other within minutes, raising the nearly dead down the hall. She tells him she lives a few miles from the hospital, that she works for Habitat for Humanity and Henry teaches at the university.

"Kids?" Sid asks.

"No," she says. Sid ducks his head and looks embarrassed, as though he had inadvertently touched a wound. She won't tell him it's by choice. Keep to the surface. "I'm afraid I don't know where Bodie is."

"You ain't alone in that." Sid laughs. "It's the other side of Yosemite. You ever been to Yosemite?"

Is there anyone in California who hasn't? she wonders. "A few times," she says. "It's beautiful."

Sid nods. "I got a special feeling for that place," he says. And then he launches into the story of meeting his wife at some church doings in Yosemite and getting married in six weeks though they were only nineteen and eighteen and how fast Louise took to the ranch and raising the kids and then the first symptoms about a year ago and two weeks ago following the ambulance over the mountain.

"It was going lickety split like it was the Indianapolis 500." He chuckles. "It's a wonder Louise lived to tell it." And then he sucks in his breath and his face collapses. "Only she won't," he says in a clotted voice. "She won't have a chance. Cancer's gone into her brain. She didn't even recognize me this morning. It like to broke my heart."

Ellen has not bargained for this. So much for the inconsequential. Serves her right for being too friendly. But she is trapped. She can't just get up and leave, not while the man is so upset. What on earth is she supposed to do?

"Um," she says, shaking her head, hoping that conveys her sympathy. Anything more would be too banal, too false.

An orderly comes through the swinging doors and stops near her. "All clear." He jerks his head back toward the ICU. Ellen doesn't immediately react. Should she leave this poor guy? "Now or never," the orderly says. "ICU closes in five minutes."

"So he's in the ICU," Sid says. "You better go on."

WHEN she enters the ICU, the nurse looks up and shrugs. The blipping machines keep blipping, the blooping sound like air bubbles rising through water keeps blooping, the intravenous drip keeps dripping. Ellen pulls a chair over to Henry's bed and picks up Henry's limp hand. His hands are elegant, the fingers long and well shaped. She raises his hand to her lips and kisses the palm and whispers, "I'm here." As she sets his hand back on the cover, she notices that his fingernails have been cut straight across. The corners are very sharp, and she fears that he might scratch himself. As though he would feel a scratch. But she will bring an emery board and smooth out those edges. That is something she can do.

AFTER her first visit to Henry next morning, Ellen goes into the alcove. Sid is there and pats the empty seat beside him and she sits down. His face asks if everything is okay, and she nods and raises her eyebrows and he nods. She's brought the morning newspaper with her and she pulls out the innards and offers him the front section. He says if it's okay he'd like the sports. Henry always looked at the front first.

The alcove slowly begins to fill up. A wispy old man in a hospital gown opened down the back comes through the swinging door from the ward, dragging an IV behind him. He sits down in a chair, his bare buttocks pressing into the slimy green vinyl cushion. No wonder they're slimy.

Sid knocks Ellen's elbow with his and gestures with his shoulder at the old man and wrinkles his nose. Ellen rolls her eyes and they exchange furtive grins of distaste. A few minutes later, a nurse pushes open the swinging door and motions to Sid. He gets up and follows her back down the hall.

Sid doesn't return to the alcove, but as Ellen enters the cafeteria for lunch she sees him talking to a cluster of men in white jackets, and in late afternoon she sees him standing at the bank of telephones, probably talking to his children, telling them the sad news.

LATE that evening Ellen passes by the alcove on the way to her last visit of the day. She glances over and there is Sid, sitting alone, his head down, the heels of his hands pressed into his eyes. She hurries on but then she goes back. He looks up at her and says, "Louise is gone."

She puts her hand on his shoulder. For a minute or two they stay like that without speaking. Then a large woman with a round pink face comes bustling through the swinging doors, waving a sheaf of papers like a flag. She says Sid should come with her to sign the documents, the releases. Sid looks at Ellen with a question, and Ellen nods and points at the floor. Sid follows the woman through the swinging door.

Ellen goes to the window and leans her head against the glass and looks out. The rain is coming down hard now. Car lights flash over the wet pavement, and the trees are swaying in the wind. Minutes tick by, and then it's too late for Ellen to go in to see Henry tonight. Henry won't know it, but he'd think she is doing the right thing, waiting for this poor man.

When Sid returns to the alcove, he smiles a weak smile and says, "Well, that's it. I guess I better start for Bodie."

Ellen imagines the long ride over Pacheco Pass and down Interstate 5, the slashing rain, and the oncoming truck lights, Sid blinded by tears. "You don't want to go back to Bodie tonight." She points toward the window. "It's really raining now, and it wouldn't be safe."

"Safe." He dismisses that with a flip of his hand. "I'd rather be bleeding like a stuck pig in a wet ditch than at that motel one more night without her." The tears start down his face and his massive shoulders rise and fall and his belly pumps in and out and he is howling like an animal. His nose begins to run and tears and mucus pool around his lips and on his chin.

"I ain't ready for this," he shouts, dragging his hand across his nose and mouth. "I ain't even got a hanky." He doesn't duck his face or try to silence himself.

Ellen reaches into her handbag and takes out the packet of tissues and hands it to him. She has never witnessed such utterly unguarded grief. She feels uneasy, even embarrassed. Yet in a way she envies him. If she let her emotions loose like that, perhaps she wouldn't feel so hard and alone.

"You can stay in our guest room," she says. "You don't have to go back to whatever that motel is."

"The goddam Honolulu," he says in a cracked voice. He begins to mop his face with a tissue. After a minute his crying subsides, and then as if Ellen's words have finally arrived, he says, "What do you mean, your guest room?"

"I mean you can stay in our guest room tonight and drive home tomorrow when it'll be safer."

Sid looks at Ellen, mulling over her offer. "You sure?" he asks.

Well, now she isn't so sure. A stranger in her house? She's been rash, downright foolish, but how hard-hearted it would be to take back her offer now. "Of course I mean it," she says, smiling. And then as though to prove that she does really mean it, she adds, "You'll have plenty of hot water right off."

Sid cocks his eyebrow. "Us regulars helping each other, huh?"

SID parks behind her in the driveway, and they run through the rain to the condo. She turns on a lamp and leads him down the hall to the guest room. He looks around the room and nods his appreciation. She shows him the adjoining bathroom and the closet where he can hang his clothes. And then she brings sheets from the linen closet.

"I can do that," Sid says, taking the sheets from her.

"Would you like anything to eat?" she asks. "I have some chicken salad that may still be okay."

"I think I'll take one of them hot showers you were talking about and then just flop," he says. "I'd probably of fallen asleep and be dead on the highway without you being so nice." He smiles. "At first I thought you were a real snoot."

SHE lies in bed, waiting for sleep, dozing, waking, spinning on images of Henry lying on the hospital bed, tied down by tubes. In half sleep, she moves across the bed, seeking Henry's warmth. "I'm here," she says. He jerks out his respirator and stands up. "I'm okay now," he says. "See?" He is wearing a tuxedo and he dances a little jig and makes a clown's face and she laughs. His eyes glow in the dim light. He rests his hand against her cheek.

"You awake?" he whispers.

It's Sid, outside her door. If she doesn't answer, perhaps he'll go away and she can slide back into her dream. It had been such a nice one. It might have ended in making love, as her dreams sometimes do. But she's wide-awake, and she knows she won't get back to sleep for a long time. She glances at the clock. 2:18. Her irritation rises. Hadn't she done all she could for this man? But then she remembers that anguished face and that howl of pain. "Give me a minute."

She puts on her robe and slippers, and she and Sid go down the hall to the living room. Sid sits on one of the chairs, and she sits opposite on the sofa. In the dim light of the lamp she sees that he has on boots and jeans and a sleeveless old-timey undershirt. The crown of his hat has left a crease in his pale red hair.

"I bet I woke you up." He looks sheepish, apologetic. "I should of taken those damn pills like the doctor said. Louise used to say sleeping was my best talent, but ever since she went into the hospital I don't sleep good at all. I just lie there and bawl." He shakes his head. "If I do get to sleep, I'm just climbing all over the bed, looking for her. It's a wonder I don't wear out the bed clothes." A little rueful smile runs across his face. "How about you? You sleep okay?"

"I sleep fine," she says. "Are you sure you won't have something to eat?" She glances across the coffee table. His expression is a little hurt, and she knows he feels rebuffed. The snoot. "To be honest, I don't sleep very well at all," she says. "I always seem to be moving in and out of some kind of half-sleep, thinking about things, maybe the hospital or maybe from years ago and then I'm dreaming or I'm drifting halfway in between."

Sid smiles. "We're always thinking about them, ain't we?"

"He removed his respirator in my dream last night and did something funny. Maybe dancing. I can't remember exactly what it was but it made me laugh." And she laughs. "Even when I was furious, he'd do something funny, maybe make a face like a little kid who's been caught with his hand in the cookie jar, and I'd have to laugh. And that would be the end of it. He didn't like to fight, at least not with me. He could always make me laugh." She pauses. "And now he's just lying there, tied down by all those tubes."

Sid reaches over and pats her knee. "We'll remember the good stuff, not all that awfulness."

She looks down at his hand. The skin is rough and hardened and the nails are ragged and chipped. A rancher's hands. Not at all like Henry's. And then she remembers she had wanted to smooth out Henry's nails so he wouldn't hurt himself. "I forgot the emery board." Her voice breaks and her eyes fill and the tears begin.

"It's about time you let up." Sid swings over to sit beside her. He pulls the tissues from his hip pocket and hands her one. "Go for it," he says. "Just go for it."

And she does go for it. The tears pour from her eyes and an awful moan rises from her throat and her body begins to tremble as though she were cold. She has lost her control, but she doesn't care. Sid won't mind. He had lost control, too, and she had seen him cry. They're the regulars. Except he won't be there in the alcove any more. His loss is already complete.

"I should be comforting you," she says in a thick voice. "I'm so sorry."

"We're comforting each other." He takes out another tissue and dabs at her face and nose. Then he puts his arm around her and pulls her against his chest and rubs her shoulder, warming her. Yes, it is comforting, she thinks, to be held by this man who understands because he's been there, too.

Slowly her crying subsides, but she doesn't move, and they don't speak. He strokes her forehead and her cheeks, and his finger traces her collarbone and moves down to the v of her robe. She smells the soap he had used when he showered and she feels her hair floating in his quickening breath.

"Jesus Christ," he says, jumping up. "What the hell am I do-ing?"

She knows what he's doing, and she doesn't want him to stop. It had been so long since anyone had touched her. She feels her own response spreading through her body, and she pulls him back to the sofa. Oh, she knows it's funny, odd, maybe wicked, two old people, strangers, beginning to make love on the sofa. But she's absolutely sure Henry and Louise would want them to comfort each other in their grief.